The Green and the Gold

Other Works by Bart Schaneman:

Trans-Siberian
Someplace Else: On Wanderlust, Expatriate Life and the Call of the Wild
The Silence is the Noise

Praise for Bart Schaneman

"Schaneman didn't write a book. He created a living, bleeding entity."

- Tanner Ballengee, author of *Sixty Tattoos I Secretly Gave Myself at Work*

"*The Green and the Gold* is a story about being stuck and the mind's amazing ability to thrash against change. Part slow and ruminating, like driving by cornfield after cornfield, and part psychological thriller, like Elena Ferrante's *Days of Abandonment*, this novel explores the innerworkings of a man who breaks free of his upbringing only to lose all sense of reality once it's gone. Schaneman shares the somber message that home isn't so much where the heart is as it is the sinking sand that one gets used to."

- Shy Watson, author of *Horror Vacui*

"Schaneman's sentences each have their own distinct realities. Carefully carved sentences creating a memorable experience of a young person learning how to be a little less young."

- Noah Cicero, author of *Las Vegas Bootlegger*

"Bart's writing elbows us into the crux of immense forces pushing and pulling at a Way Of Life across rural Plains places."

- Rich Baiocco, author of *Death in a Rifle Garden*

ISBN: 978-1-951226-09-1

Cover Art: Detail from *The Veteran in a New Field* by Winslow Homer

Published by Trident Press
940 Pearl St.
Boulder, CO 80302
tridentcafe.com/trident-press-titles

THE GREEN AND THE GOLD

by Bart Schaneman

Trident Press
Boulder, CO

FOREWORD

The first time I read *The Green and the Gold* was an early manuscript copy Bart mailed to the small bayside house I was renting for the summer in Virginia. This was 2005, the heart of July, and the book was in the hands of a rep at Grove Press. The story of the book's acquisition was the stuff of legend to people we knew. Bart sent the venerable publishing house a copy and said something along the lines of, "I know you don't take unsolicited manuscripts and I don't have an agent, but you should take a chance on a young writer because that's something you *used* to do." Bart dropped the challenge and Grove accepted. Grove! The house of Kerouac and Burroughs, of Frank O'Hara and Camus and D.H. Lawrence and Bertolt Brecht and fucking Henry Miller's goddamn *Tropic of Cancer*. It felt (and was, and still is) huge.

Bart's rep at Grove championed the book and worked back and forth on edits then disappeared entirely (and suddenly) when she left the company. That was enough, however, to make Bart's manuscript notorious amongst our friends. He'd missed his shot with Grove, but they wanted it. They fucking *wanted* it, and they took him on without an agent. The idea of it was enough to give hope to any young writer with a little guts and self-confidence. (In our young 20s we had plenty of both.)

The summer I read Bart's manuscript I spent driving my beat-to-shit Volvo down to the Chesapeake Bay each morning to swim then back home for a few hours work on my own first book about my own hometown followed by an afternoon reading Bart's work—reading it then rereading it; pouring over lines like, "At the beginning of winter the days waned and the landscape changed from gold and green to brown and gray." Reading, and feeling the life and the music in sections like: "As we stood before it, we saw it become the color of communication, of honesty, of a train to the ocean, a sign changed from open to closed, a commitment to peace, riding horses, a neighborhood buried in snow..." That particular part (and the lines that followed) filled me with an energy I'd not yet felt. It is a paragraph I return to often, all these years later, and a paragraph that continues to influence how I write and what I consider "good."

I loved *The Green and the Gold* profoundly and I studied it because I knew reading it (and *knowing* it) would make my own first book better. It did, but Bart's novel remains a far better first book. We were very young then, but he'd found a thing I hadn't—a mainline to his own powers, a rare connection to the circuity of FEELING and LIFE. There is a beating heart at the center of this story; the words jump from the sentences as if lit by some inner fire, the sentences electrical, vibrating like the metal wheels of a train upon their metal track, beating a rhythm that is the rhythm of America—a rhythm of highways, small towns, tractors and harvesters in fields, the gray shroud of a blizzard on the horizon, of oil derricks pumping, and black tornados turning like screws in the charging sky. Reading Bart's manuscript in the summer of 2005 felt like good things coming, wilder life, power without agenda, real truth. Fucking hell. Sign me up. Plug me the goddamn fuck IN.

The Green and the Gold is the story of a young man trying his damnedest to deal with the changing terrain of life. It's about the small town he grew up in, and the larger one he went off to for college. It is a very Midwestern book and because of that it is the most American kind of book. *The Green and the Gold* is a story of quiet winter days, frozen interstates, troubled love, work, fevers, sex, basement parties, horses, cattle, corn fields and soy fields, cowboys, college kids, and farm families. Growing up in San Diego before moving to Virginia, the hometown I knew was skate punks and beach goths, crystal meth and taco shops. His was absolutely exotic. Through Bart's writing, I came to mythologize and worship the Middlewest.

I left Virginia that summer to move to Portland, but when I left Portland four years after that, I left it for the Midwest. I had high hopes for a sweet, virtuous place, a place where everyone was either Bart Schaneman or Conor Oberst, a place of hard workers and straight-shooters. I was wrong in expecting something so definitively good. (In 2009, when I finally got to the Midwest, the bad people were out there, but they didn't have flags and signs in their yard. It would be a few years before the racists, fascists, and bigots began to rise. In 2021 they are still a dominant force.) Nevertheless, Bart tells the truth about middle-America in his book. After a decade here I can say in all confidence that he wrote *The Green and the Gold* with authority. Is the Midwest of 2021 a different Midwest than that of the early 2000s? Without question, but the truth in this novel is still there. To me, for a very long time, the Midwest was Bart Schaneman's *The Green and the Gold* and Bright Eyes' *Lifted*. At its best, it still is.

Today is the first day of spring after a long winter and a year of grappling with life on COVID lockdown, the virus chewing its way through our towns and cities like a rat in the walls. It's a very dark night here on the Ruby Teeth Homestead, the moon behind the clouds, and with the windows open you can hear the chorus of frogs trilling gently down at the pond and the breeze rustling the branches of the oak and old maples. Rereading Bart Schaneman's book tonight feels like a good omen for the year ahead. As the world comes back to life after too long buried in ice, *The Green and the Gold*, a novel so steeped in winter, seems to welcome it.

-Adam Gnade
Ruby Teeth Homestead, rural Midwest, 3/20/2021

SCOTTSBLUFF I

I

The house shrank during the short time I was gone. It seemed now we kept the curtains drawn, closed the windows, and never went outside. It was hard to sleep but harder to feel alive. I moved like an echo through the house, the hollow, empty reverberation of a once bolder sound. Dad and I spoke when there was no other choice. He used direct and informal language and spoke without looking. Mom and I got along better. She was compassionate still, the only way she could ever be, but there was no happiness in her voice. They were disappointed in me and I tried not to get in their way.

On a Saturday morning he came into my room without knocking, turning on my light then walking out of my room, leaving the door open. After I dressed, on the table the coffee and rolls were cold so I poured milk over sugar and cereal. A dull malaise remained behind my eyes, and I stared across the table at the newspaper on the other end.

We lived on Lake Minatare about ten miles from Scottsbluff. It was a man made lake and the biggest one in the area. They were all about empty then, though—there was little water that year, the result of a two-year drought and no snowfall in the mountains. So we found ourselves living on the shore of what was closer to a puddle.

Recreation did not suffer much. It was a state park and they retained enough water to support the natural habitat and enough to allow people to jet ski and boat. Plus there was more than enough sand for four-wheelers and dune buggies. But the farmers without wells and sprinklers watched their bank accounts roll back and their hollowed cheeks sink deeper. Without water from the canals, only those lucky enough to have tapped into the aquifer could hope to grow anything.

In Scottsbluff the hometown stores and non-corporate businesses slowly went broke and some boarded up their windows. No agriculture, no money. Scottsbluff was a farm town of fourteen thousand in the middle of the plains. As you leave the town you see fields—a farmhouse with a barn and some trees set back in a cornfield every mile or so. You might see a white or green tractor out in that field, a farmer working for a little bit of nothing.

Out on the lake full-grown oak and cottonwood trees surrounded the water, hanging their branches over the surface, dropping in leaves when the wind blew right. One of the ancient oaks grew through the center of our wooden deck that ran around the brick and gray-sided building we lived in. Our modest house was well kept by my parents' efforts. Something they could more easily control.

On most Saturday mornings my parents doubled their enthusiasm. They were good about that, always wanting to make the most of their time. We went everywhere together. To the park, to the supercenter, on group outings with my grandmother to the zoo. That day was my deceased grandfather Harry's one-year anniversary so we were meeting my grandmother and aunt and uncle at the cemetery.

Granddad Harry wrote in his will that he wanted to be buried out in the country. Somewhere where the light at night came from the stars and the moon. Harry made a living as a banker who loved art and the outdoors when he wasn't pooling people's money. An amateur outdoorsman and painter, he spent his weekends pheasant hunting or fishing but liked more than anything to hole himself up in his studio with the windows open and a blank easel. He would spend so much time in his studio that Grandmother brought him his meals while he painted, wiping his hands off on his apron then washing them in the sink. Granddad painted for himself and most of the family never knew what he made with his brush, only Grandmother was allowed to peak at his canvas in glimpses she stole when she brought him sandwiches.

A small part Native American, Granddad also made it a point to educate himself about the culture of his tribe, but which one he was descendant of escapes me—he didn't talk much about it with the rest of us. There were feathers and leather vests on the wall of his studio, but without a proper education I never understood their significance. It was well known in the family that he read about the history of the Native American and left on occasional weekends to practice some of the rituals.

With imagined pictures of his guns and feathers on the wall, him standing in front of an easel, I sat in the back seat of our car and shut my door. We didn't have that far to drive to the cemetery—it was down a gravel road about three miles from the lake. We passed a tractor and grain cart on the road and the man waved with one finger and my father waved back.

At the cemetery on the corner of two dirt roads, the field of gravestones spread out across a flat, green, grassy space and they were protected by a row of pine trees bordering the field. The graveyard was small, half of a football field, and the gravestones were simple slabs of stone not taller than waist-high. There were no crypts or walk-in graves.

First to arrive, we parked on the side of the dirt road next to the cemetery and shut our doors softly. He was Mom's dad and we followed her to the gravestone. My uncle had planted a sapling next to the plot the week after the burial so we knew where to go. Mom brought a bouquet of flowers and she set the vase next to the stone. Carved into the gravestone were his name and date and a picture of a dove, a bird he often painted.

A cloud of dust rose in the distance and we knew that it was my grandmother with my aunt and uncle. They parked behind our car. She wept as she walked past us, carrying one red rose, and laid it down across the front of the stone. We all cried except Dad, who stood silent, observing.

When we got home we split up. He went into his study, she went to the laundry room, and I went to the front yard. It was a weekend day on the lake and there were boats in the water—skiers behind the ski boats and fishing poles sticking out of the fishing boats—making smooth wakes as they passed our yard. I watched a boy and a girl on a jet ski in lifejackets laughing, her arms wrapped around his waist, jumping the wake behind a motorboat.

A few years ago, Dad built a wooden dock that was good for fishing, and it sounded good to try and catch a fish. Fishing, a creative and destructive act, would satisfy two of my nagging urges. We kept the poles in the shed with the boat.

Turning on the shed light I became aware of the cardboard boxes in the corner at the nose of the boat. They sat against the far wall stacked three high. When Granddad died Grandmother moved in with my aunt and uncle. They didn't have room to keep all of her and Granddad's possessions and she couldn't bear to sell them. So we took some of his stuff and stored it in our garage.

My automatic reel fishing pole worked but I wanted to graduate to an actual reel cast pole, to learn to fish without just pushing a button. I must have been inspired by all those thoughts of the outdoorsman. Granddad could fly-fish as well as any man I ever watched.

All of Granddad's poles were in one of the boxes; I knew because I helped to pack them into one of the trunks. I took off the tarp and moved the small boxes off the bigger ones buried on the bottom. There were three or four trunks that looked the same and the first one I opened was all of his painting supplies. The next one held some of his paintings. I began taking them from the box and setting them up against the boat to look at his work.

The first painting in the box was of Grandmother. A portrait he painted of her when she was in her thirties. Her hair was long, brown, and straight and she was pretty. I set this on a box to look at the next one. It was a painting of a hawk lifting a mouse from a field. Pretty standard painting really. The next painting wasn't though. It was different. The canvas filled the trunk, about five and a half feet by four feet, and painted on it were two blocks of solid color stacked flush on top of each other. I took the painting out to take a closer look at it.

Granddad hadn't covered the entire painting with oil. The edges remained unpainted, fuzzy and whitish around the border. The top block was a deep purple, almost black, like the color of a plum, and the bottom block was jet black with blue edges fading into the white. The blocks seemed to float on the white of the canvas. It seemed unfinished to me, but far more interesting than the rest of the paintings—under that painting was a detailed rendering of a pheasant.

I took the purple and black painting, climbed up onto the boat, and sat down with it. It was awkward and large and I set it down to look at. Then, thinking I should preserve the rest of the paintings from dust, I went down and put them back in the trunk but left the one I was interested in up on the boat. When I closed the lid of the trunk, I noticed there was black paint on my hands. I thought the painting must not have been all the way dry, which meant that Granddad was still working on it before—

A weird thing happened then. After I closed the other three paintings in the trunk, when I went up to the boat to check the wetness of the paint, what I thought had been a black block of color at the bottom now appeared to me as royal blue. I looked at my hands and the paint was also not black but blue. I touched the painting with my free hand to check the wetness and nothing else came off. I picked it up then turned it over. Written on the back of the canvas, the words read, "The paint of my blood shall reflect the color of your soul." That didn't make any sense. I thought about it for a minute but the two blocks of color started to bore me. The whole painting seemed a little simplistic.

Setting the painting up against the wheel of the boat trailer, the fishing poles were still what interested me and they were easily removed from the box. Before leaving the shed the painting came into view but nothing seemed to have changed, it was still purple over blue.

For most of the day, the fish stayed alive, out of danger from my hook hanging down from the front of the dock. The water was smooth and because the shores were so receded I could see across the lake. Boats crossed paths, teenagers on jet skis, people reclining in yellow and black doughnut inner tubes. Above the ridge that rose up behind the lake, the line from a white jet stream grew wider as it cut across the sky, the jet pulling a white, widening piece of cotton thread. The spreading flyover lines were the white stripes that triggered a Midwesterner's dreams. I imagined people flying to the coasts and looking out the windows down at the field formations much like staring at a tile mosaic. They looked out across our part of the country as though seeing thousands and thousands of my Grandfather's painting.

From my hand, the silver line that fell from my pole remained loose as the sun tanned the tops of my thighs. Most of the water from the lake was gone, and it was shallow around the posts that held up the dock. There weren't many days left in the year for boating. It always became like that during the fall, but this year was worse. In a typical year the water came down from the mountains and they filled the lake, slowly sending it into the fields, the green plants turning the water into yellow corn kernels or white beans. Golden wheat and green alfalfa. Most of the beans would be gone, harvested with red tractors and taken with trucks to the elevators. But the corn would still be ripening, yellowing in the fields and between the sky and the lake, the golden stalks remaining on the plains. In a normal year.

Heavy footsteps came up behind me.

Dad smiled softly then took the pole from me and cast effortlessly into the water. He handed it back then walked toward the house. There was no more interaction than that, as if he would have me learn something for myself. A foreign concept yet to be introduced by him. Practicing the finger thing for a while led me to tangling the line into a ball of plastic that there was no way would ever come undone.

Giving his lesson a chance to sink in, I decided to retire the fishing pole. The door of the shed pulled open with a little effort, spreading light on the boat. At that moment the pole fell from my hand with a small sound. At the tire of the boat, on the painting, the purple block was unchanged, it remained dark, but under it the blue had turned to a deep, crimson red. Kneeling down my hand touched the paint and a little bit of red came off onto my finger tip. A red dot on my now red finger. In the illuminated garage the single naked light bulb was enough that the painting showed up clear—the bottom block lost all of its blue and changed to red.

After a little more inspection, the painting went into the trunk for the rest of the afternoon. Tall thunderheads formed up over the west side of the lake and moved toward the water, so all the boats went to shore or docked. The people leaving the water for fear of lightning. The wind loudened but the trees shook off few leaves. Out across the water, crests of whitecaps spotted the lake. It would be an hour before the rain but the wind announced its presence. I rubbed my thumb against the dried red paint on my finger as I watched the clouds form.

I was on the dock, lying on my back, when the rain started. The first few drops on my forehead felt cool and good. The rain increased, streaking the air in white lines, the water soaking through my clothes.

That night, after the rain and dinner with my parents, I went out to the shed. They kept all the keys to the cars in their room so they felt okay letting me leave the house. The naked light bulb shone meager rays of light onto the trunk. My feet moved soft on the concrete floor of the shed in an attempt to avoid questions from my parents about what I was doing in there—the painting already a secret. After the lid of the trunk opened with an effort, the light was too weak so I brought the color blocks out and onto the workbench at the side of the boat. The colors remained purple over red but the red was of a lighter shade. My finger lifted paint from the blocks before they were returned to the trunk.

When I went to bed that night I stayed up thinking about my Grandfather and the painting and how he must have known some type of Indian magic that gave the painting its power. I imagined him mixing the paint with the blood from his fingers. Then I told myself that had to be false. I didn't believe in magic. I tried to sleep but there was something there, something I believed about it. There must have been because even though the lid of the trunk remained unopened for weeks, the secret also remained closed within me.

2

At the beginning of winter the days waned and the landscape changed from gold and green to brown and gray. Life retreated into caves to wait it out. On a Sunday night Dad, Mom, and I sat in the living room watching a news program on the television and a show came on about the war. The broadcaster gave a body count from a suicide bombing but showed no images of the dead.

"Maybe you should join the Army," he said, folding down his newspaper. "They'll teach you a few things."

Under my sinuses and through my temples a tightness squeezed until it spread down into my throat.

"What is he going to do?" he said. "I'm going to work tomorrow and so are you. And I don't think it's a good idea to leave him here alone."

The television then switched to coverage of nighttime war—glowing green streaks of light trailing behind the bombs. My mother looked over at me from the couch. I was sitting on a chair at the other end of the room from him with her between us. He picked up the phone and dialed a number.

"Hello. Bill? Yes, yes like a dog. No, I don't think anytime soon. Look, Bill, the reason I'm calling is my son Carrick's in town for a while and he's got some time on his hands. Would you mind if he came over and gave you a hand? I know you've got plenty of work. No. No. None of that. No, he's not that at all. Okay? You sure you don't mind? Okay. Seven. He'll be there."

The morning I started at Bill's Mom made a big breakfast of

pancakes and bacon but all the bacon went to them. I don't eat bacon and didn't say a word as we ate. Dad gave me good advice.

"Don't slack. Work fast. Hustle. Johnson's a hard worker but he's close to forty years older than you."

He took me to the closet and gave me a pair of his old coveralls, brown with a hole on the thigh from a branding iron. They were too big and my shoulders didn't fit, but they weren't too long—I was as tall as my father—so I could walk in them. Mom packed me a lunch in a small plastic cooler and that went with me. We got in the Jeep and he continued to advise me on proper manual labor techniques.

Johnson lived a mile to the south of us in a two-bedroom house. There was a large steel shed behind the house and green tractors next to it. A silver grain silo stood before a cement feed bunk and a stretch of fence for a cattle corral. There was a small shed on the other side of the yard and a larger barn. There was another house behind the barn where the migrant workers had stayed in the past, but there were no migrant workers anymore, none that lived on the farms anyway, so the farmer filled the house with used tires. Bill's house was small, white, with a green-shingled roof. A brownish-tan lawn wrapped around the front and sides, a white propane tank at one end and a red, miniature windmill at the other. At the entrance to the yard were five evergreen pine trees and a mailbox.

Bill had never been married and everyone wondered what was wrong with him, some thought him defective. But he grew good crops. They usually yielded as good as or better than any of his neighbors, so the people respected his efforts. Everyone said he just worked too much to have time for anyone else.

I was about ten the only time we actually met. Bill had forgotten to shut a gate, he said the cattle pushed it open but Dad said Bill left it open, and a hundred or so of his black Angus escaped, spread out all across the fields and crossed the highway down to the lake. We didn't really meet, I guess—he almost ran me over with his horse when I mounted my little white four-wheeler steed to help out but instead cut him off. One of his heifers ran in the lake and drowned that day.

So he really didn't know me when Dad dropped me off in his yard. He came down from the feed truck as he made it to the end of the cement bunk of the corral with the truck. He walked over to the driver's side of my Dad's Jeep.

"You sure you don't mind, Bill?"

"Heck no. It's fine. If you're sure you don't mind me stealing all your help." Bill looked at me and smiled. "You eat your Wheaties this morning son?"

I smiled a little.

"I'll pick him up after I get off work," Dad said.

"You still down at the feedlot?"

"Until I win the lottery."

"Sixteen mil this week."

"I'm stopping by the station to pick up my tickets on my way to work. Maybe I won't have to even go in today," Dad said, then he turned and looked at me. "Work hard."

"Don't worry about pickin' him up. I'll drop him off before dark."

Bill took my lunch from me and put it in his porch. Dad drove out of the yard and my eyes followed him.

"C'mon, son. Lots to do," Bill said, patting my shoulder.

Bill led me to the end of the yard by the straw stack. The day was blue and gray and cold, the sun shining for light but not for heat. Weather stations forecasted snow on the way so Bill wanted to put straw in for the cattle before we started on the fence.

"I'll get the loader over here. Grapple's broke so we'll have to fill it ourselves."

Yellow, rectangle, orange-twined straw bales were stacked twelve high and Bill wanted them down from the top. Stacked in an alternating pattern, they were easy to climb. I waited at the top of the stack until Bill drove the loader over and set the bucket about halfway up.

"Throw 'em down into the bucket," he called up from the loader. "They stack better lengthwise."

The straw was dry and light and the bales lifted easy. Bill and I loaded then dumped five loads into the corral. We went in with knives and cut the twines. The cattle knew what the straw was and when we cut the orange twine and moved on they would go to the bales and butt them with their heads, spreading it themselves, speeding up the process. We had two pitchforks and used them to spread it where the cattle didn't until the soft yellow blades of straw blanketed the cold dirt of the corral.

At first I hated the work. It seemed so pointless. But as the day went on I felt a lot better about it. It took my mind off everything I was ashamed of, everything that made me feel guilty about what I thought then were my bad decisions. The harder I worked the warmer I got, so I kept moving as much as I could. My hands and ears were burning from the increasing wind but my core kept warm, the morning sun bright and rising.

We walked through the metal gate and it wasn't ten minutes after we left the pen that the cattle were curled up in the straw, some rolling on their sides and snorting. Bill led us over to a trailer with a pile of metal fence posts.

"We need to clean out the grain silo but first we're going out to put up fence. I'll get the truck. You hook up the hitch on the trailer."

Bill got in his rusted silver pickup and pumped the accelerator until the engine was primed then he started it and drove up to the trailer. I did my best to impersonate an air traffic controller as he backed the pickup toward the trailer hitch. The silver ball on the bumper of the pickup didn't look low enough to fit under the hitch of the trailer so I told Bill to hold on as I cranked up the jack. But the trailer was high enough, because I cranked the jack up until the trailer tilted and some of the poles slid off the back and the hitch flew into the air. Bill stopped the truck and watched as I got onto the front of the trailer, standing on it, and used all my weight to get it down. The seesaw needed someone heavier on the end.

After my weight shifted the trailer down he backed up, with me giving him the wave, and the ball lined up under the dome and I cranked the trailer down. The ball pushed out a metal piece that snapped into place after it fit into the dome of the trailer hitch. The wheel at the end of the jack spun as I cranked the wheel and it cleared the ground.

"Get it?"

"Where's the pin?"

Bill found the pin to secure the jack and slipped the key into the hole at the end.

"Let me throw those poles on," I said as I ran to the back of the trailer.

"Thought you were going to flip it over. Get away from you?"

"Don't know my own strength."

"Don't know how to run a jack you mean?"

That was more the case.

I picked up the thin metal poles and threw them onto the trailer.

"Get in."

Inside Bill's truck smelled of soil. Not dust but the moist smell of a fresh handful of clay. The floorboards were layered in an inch of brown dirt and pebbles that crunched underfoot. The dashboard wasn't much better, cracked and streaked from fingers wiping at the dust. A small two-year-old calendar with a picture of a girl in a swimsuit hung above the radio. Then there was Bill, driving with one hand on the bottom of the steering wheel and smiling at me as he talked.

"Glad to have you here, Carrick. Can use a little help. A guy goes crazy all by himself."

My days in Lincoln confirmed the truth of that statement.

"We're going to take these posts up to the top corner and

string the wire. The ground's not too frozen so they should go in all right. I'll show you how to use the post pounder. It's not all that difficult as long as you get 'em started straight."

All the black cattle were in the pens on the straw. They ate corn stalks in the winter after the harvest, cleaning up what the combines missed.

"We'll fence from the gate all around the sixty. Should have enough wire, don't know if we'll have enough posts though. We'll just do what we can. I think Harold's got some extras."

Harold was Bill's brother and a rancher more than a farmer. He owned more cattle than Bill and lived on the other side of the lake where the dry soil only grew pasture grass.

When Bill stopped the truck at the end of the corral we got out and went to the trailer. It was mid-morning by then and the sun warmed our skin. The problems from before lessened out there in the cold air and warm sun—everything was too simple to cause a lot of worry.

The work went good. We worked amid the chopped yellow stalks of a harvested cornfield. Out in the middle of the field an orange oilwell pumped up and down like a seesaw. Once he showed me how to work the pounder, Bill would drive while I put in the posts. I'd take one from the trailer, slide the insulator down, and slide the heavier, iron post-pounder over the thin metal and heave it up and down until the wedge that was welded onto the bottom of the post like backwards arrow feathers was completely pounded into the dirt. Then I'd get on the trailer and we'd drive ten yards and I'd get off and do another.

We worked until noon then went to the house and got our lunches. The field was about half-done. I guessed I wasn't that efficient but was getting better as time went on. Bill said it had gone good. I wasn't sure I believed him. I hadn't been good at anything in a long time.

Bill's house was old and dirty, not that different from him. He kept a cat inside and that might have had something to do with it. The yard was full of feral ones, twenty or so that lived in the barn and he didn't want the one in the house to either go wild or be eaten by the ones that were. There wasn't a spot in the house that didn't have cat hair on it, but as much as I've never liked cats, it didn't bother me all that much. If I was as old as Bill I would want something, anything, to keep me from sticking my head in an auger. Since I'd been home I was having the old dream again.

We ate lunch at the table, me unwrapping my sandwich and apple, Bill heating up some soup on the stovetop. Bill didn't have cable but he owned a television so we watched the only thing on during the middle of the day: soap operas. We didn't talk much as we ate and I felt our setup becoming awkward. Maybe he didn't think all that much of me. Maybe he didn't want me in his house. Maybe he was embarrassed. I thought about that a little and decided it was more the last thing than anything. That was why he wasn't talking to me, because he was embarrassed. But no way, he'd been living like this his entire life. There was no way he felt uncomfortable every time someone came over. Unless no one ever came over. And I was the first visitor he'd entertained in a long time and he didn't know how to act. I didn't know what to say about the situation. We needed an icebreaker.

But none came. We watched television without talking until we finished our lunch. Then Bill turned off the TV.

"Ready to go put the rest in?" he asked.

We went out and worked harder this time. The food gave us strength and the sun kept us warm. It was windy but there wasn't dust so we could go on without much trouble. The rest of the afternoon went well, Bill driving, me pounding posts, and by the time we got around the field the sky grew gray and dark. Bill told me to get in the truck and we went to the yard as dusk set in.

"You coming back tomorrow?" he asked.

"Sure. This was good."

"I'll leave the trailer on then. We can run the wire...hey, I know. We can take the car. You ever driven in an Aston Martin?"

"Nope."

"Oh boy, you're in for a treat. It's in the shed. We'll have to take off the cover but I keep it runnin' so it should start just fine."

On the other side of the yard from the house there was a small, white wooden shed. The doors were held closed with a plank of wood and Bill slid it back. I could see a smile in his eye. He pulled open the doors and laughed a little to himself.

He moved a lawnmower out of the way and behind it was a short car under a brown, dust-covered tarp. The tarp created a cloud of dust when we swept off the cover. A white, two-seater roadster gleamed in what little light was left.

"I'll pull it out," he said. "You shut the doors behind me."

It groaned a little but started on the first try and Bill honked once as he drove it out of the shed. I pulled the shed doors shut and ran to open my door.

"Get in!"

He honked twice as we took off out of the yard. We sped down the dirt road away from his house until we were gone a couple miles, then, at an intersection he turned left and headed that way for a mile until he came to the highway. Two horses with their heads over the fence jumped and ran off when they heard us coming. Then we turned left and sped up. There wasn't a heater in that thing and it was full of holes, but neither Bill nor I cared because it was loud and the whole experience was as rewarding after a full day of work as we could want. A nice, relaxed, super loud drive.

We could see my house coming up and I felt like I was five again; I didn't want the drive to end. Bill slowed down to ease into our driveway.

"You're home, Carrick. Same time tomorrow?"

"I'll talk to my Dad and we'll see what he wants to do."

"Would love to have you."

I didn't say anything.

"All right then," Bill said. "Have yourself a good night. Get some sleep. Stringin' wire in the mornin'."

The roadster sputtered out of the driveway and he honked again. Watching him leave left me feeling good. The day with Bill made me happy and I was sure it had made him feel the same. But then I turned and opened the door to the house and everything that Bill helped me forget came back. Hands squeezed around my neck.

Ever since I came home Mom and Dad adopted this stance with me, this indifference and unwillingness to be anything other than unhappy whenever in the same room. As if they punished themselves at the same time they punished me, making it twice as heavy and guilt-ridden on my end.

After hanging my coveralls on the hook in the hallway by the door, I walked into the kitchen. Mom browned hamburger in a skillet on the stovetop. She didn't turn around though she had heard me when the front door opened and shut.

I walked into the family room and Dad sat on his chair reading the newspaper and watching the news. The newscaster reported on a volcano in Hawaii. A tidal wave sounded nice. When the news went to commercial he folded down his paper and looked over at me.

"Did you mess anything up?"

"No."

He nodded once. That was it and all I could get myself to say. The weather forecast the weatherman gave showed a sun partly covered by a cloud. I fell asleep on the couch.

The next morning it still hadn't snowed and Dad took me over to Bill's. When we drove into the yard he came out of his house and smiled with the energy and health my family forgot. They took everything as serious as death. Bill neither knew nor cared about my problem, it wasn't his and so he became a good escape from it all. He would tell me stories and jokes and we would laugh about the good things, the things that didn't matter.

We strung wire that morning, tying the silver thread to a post at the end of the field then driving a tractor along the line of post we pounded. I followed the tractor and hooked the wire to the insulators and Bill drove slow, not saying anything, just listening to the sound of the spool of wire unrolling behind the tractor and the slow chug of the engine. The weather held the same, a little windy and the sky was gray, but the sun came out in the middle of the day and warmed everything, working a little, before lying down in a field of clouds. Every day was shorter than the last.

Dad and Bill agreed I would be paid five dollars an hour, no taxes, no W-2 forms, just straight-up, under the table wages. He paid me every Friday and the money didn't go anywhere but in a wad folded up in my sock drawer. I had no car and no friends, no place to go to spend it.

So we worked six days a week and the first month of that went fast. The mornings came early and the nights ended short. In between I would learn so much from Bill about the farm and living on your own that I would be tired enough to sleep easy until waking up in the cold of the post-dawn hour.

It wasn't a month into working with Bill that I decided I wanted his life. There was so much about it that was good. He lived out in the country, did what he wanted, worked his own hours, could come and go as he pleased, no boss, no rules, didn't have to go to school, was just smart enough to get done what he needed to get done. Any problem he dealt with could be solved with his hands and his head, in that order, if the latter was even necessary.

After we strung out all the wire and hooked it to the insulators, we hooked up a charger to a power line and connected it to the fence. The fencer had a light that was built in so you could check the charge to make sure the fence was electrified. We hooked it up but the light didn't come on.

"It must be grounded, touching somewhere," Bill said.

We got in his truck and went looking for a spot where the wire fell into the corn stalks. The short, pale yellow stalks, less than knee high, bristled up in rows. Leaves from the stalks covered the ditches in between. We drove along the road on the edges of the field, following the posts.

"Watch the wire and if it looks like it's touching the post or a stalk we have to get out and fix it."

This was the biggest kind of problem he ever dealt with in a day.

"Hey Bill, I'm looking, but do you mind if I ask you something?"

"Sure shoot."

"Would you trade your life for anything?"

"Would I trade my life for anything? That's quite the question this morning Carrick. What's on your mind?"

"Nothing. I just want to know. I mean you seem to be somehow, I don't know, *born* to do this. You know how to handle everything."

"This is all I know how to do."

"But you're a smart guy. You could have learned to do something else. Anything you ever wanted to do."

"Nope. Didn't ever want to do anything else. This was all I ever knew how to do. The only thing I was good at. I always figured a guy should do what he was good at and stick with that one thing."

"Sure, but you know, I mean you never got married, never even lived in a city. Don't you think you should have tried your hand at something else? Tried to make it in a harsher environment?"

"Boy these elements out here are harsh enough for anyone. Plus, you've got to be crazy to go looking for something like that."

The wire rose and fell from post to post but remained taut.

"Maybe, but you know...I guess I don't know what I'm getting at."

"You're young is all. You're full of ideas and ambitions. I was like you once. I know how you're thinking."

"No, that's not it. I don't want the skyscraper job or to be some office monkey. Not that. I just, I don't know, I feel like I need to go see something. That the world's a big place, you know?"

"Are you watching that wire?"

"It looks good. It's still up."

"Keep your eye on it."

"I got it."

I watched as we passed the silver thread. Watching it go up and down from insulator to insulator, the cables on the Golden Gate bridge.

"How come you're not married, if you don't mind me asking?"

"Boy. Wooeee. All the big questions this morning. Boy, what you'd you eat for breakfast? I'm going to have to tell your Mom to keep the sugar off your Wheaties."

"Just curious is all."

"No, it's okay. I get asked that question a lot. 'You're a likeable enough guy Bill, how come you're not married? How'd a good guy like you go this far in life without some girl getting eyes for you?' And to tell you the truth Carrick, there's no real reason. I guess I would just say I blew it a lot growing up. I mean I had a lot of great girlfriends. This one. Jess. She was something. But I never thought until I was older that I would be alone my whole life. I'm not sure why son but I thought there would always be someone to date. Didn't turn out that way though."

"No way. There's no way that you're one of those lessons. One of those guys that you see in the movies that tells the teenager find yourself a girl who loves you and hold onto her and never let go. Never let her go!"

"Now be careful, Carrick. You don't know what you're talking about."

"You want to teach me some lesson about life and love?"

"Careful son."

"Oh god. Are you serious? You think I'm really going to buy into that?"

"Are you watching that wire?"

"I mean you've got to be happy here. You have the most peaceful existence known to man. You always hear people talking about the serenity of working the land and how you work with your hands, about how good it is for the soul."

"All that doesn't mean nothing if you've got nobody to share it with."

"What? Whatever. You mean you don't have anyone to tell you what to do."

"No. Watch the wire."

"Hey, stop. It's down."

3

On Friday nights when Bill would say "get out of here, go paint the town," I would take his car and drive home. Home to the lake and the barren branches rising up from the trees like fingers reaching for the light at the top. When it darkened I usually stayed in and read books, rubbing my feet together to keep them warm. I would stay up late in my room with the lights on and the walls squeezing shut, tighter the later it got, expecting to look up and find the ceiling resting on my chest.

When I slept I dreamed the same dream over and over. It started simple, a summer day with my friends on a ditchbank. In high school we went to this spot with a tree next to a ditchbank road where we overlooked the airport and the rest of the city. We usually went there at night to drink and try to kiss girls but this was a different dream. The one I had that night went like *Carrick toss that over...to focus on...what girl...Gwen...Ha, but then SEE I TOLD YOU you CAN get it a lot of...did you see that? No, up there, look...no. NO. Not again. Hurry up, they're coming. There's ANOTHER ONE did you see that? OH GOD. They're coming, hurry, HURRY. GET IN let's go Just leave, they're fast, oh, but if you don't go now, C'MON, CARRICK, get up, get up just GET UP, they've got engines. THEY'VE GOT JETS. We need to get in the canal, they won't find us there, C'MON JUST JUMP, screw this, stay, I'm going. Stay and die. I'm jumping, you have to go NOW, they're here, they're everywhere. White paint on a domed nose, a man with a black mustache holding the controls, the sun glaring off the cockpit, the spinning blades.*

This was my recurring dream. The one I always had. Sometimes I jumped into the canal and woke up, sometimes I stood frozen waiting for death, then woke up, and sometimes I died.

One Friday Mom told me to take the car to town to pick up the dry cleaning. I stopped at the record store instead. It wasn't until that night that I began longing for the Friday sun to fall. We went to high school together but she was two years older; I didn't know her well enough and never had the heart to ask her what she was still doing in Scottsbluff, working at Budget Music.

The store was one of four others in a mini-mall next to a car dealership. I walked in and looked around a little bit, stopping to slap back the plastic jewel cases in the soundtrack section. I kept moving until I noticed the guitars on the wall. She came over then. I've been in a love with one person or another since I was twelve, but we didn't hit it off immediately.

She walked over to the counter. My eyes followed her from where I stood. A morning sun rose over a mountain. The guitars hung from the wall, electric, acoustic, and with the money from Bill I took the cheapest black acoustic down by the neck and to the counter.

She scanned the tag and found the box.

"Maribel," she held out her hand. It was soft. "I play too. We should play sometime."

She wrote down her number on the receipt and put it in the cardboard box my guitar came in, throwing in a chord book.

I didn't return to Budget for a while but I took my guitar home and played. The blisters took a while to form and I played in my room when I could. I played with the chord book—there wasn't much about other people's songs that I wanted to concern myself with. I really only wanted to play what I wrote. The lyrics weren't good, but they did improve. I wrote a lot about California with a simple C, A minor, G chord progression.

For me to get any better I practiced as much as I could. At first, before I developed the dexterity and the blisters, I took my own advice. I realized that there were choices I could make. Choices about fate, about predestination, about wrestling control, about hacking it all away. I went to the store to get some picks and a book of songs to learn how to play.

When I walked in the store was empty. Maribel was labeling albums. I moved closer, following her as she worked. She put the gun down and smiled.

"I thought you were going to call me," she said. "Can I help you with something?"

She took me over to a slotted plastic case and went through a bunch of different types, this one for finger picking, this one goes on your thumb, these are the thin kind, these are thick. As she handed me a type to feel I noticed there was a tattoo of a dolphin on the underside of her wrist.

Suddenly we were picked up and the carpet became a rising wave carrying us to Hawaii, dropping us gently down on the white sand. We stood under palm trees watching the waves rise up and curl over a reef break, coming down in white sections, the white water foaming toward the shore.

Neither one of us were doing anything with our hands. I noticed the songbooks and walked over. I was cautious when I looked at the books. Most pop artists I'd never want to learn from—there's enough of that in the world.

She walked over to the counter, took some paper off the wall at the register and wrote down some capital letters under the song's name.

You know this song I'm sure. The strumming pattern's really easy. It's almost all down strums. The only chord that might be kind of hard for you is the F but once you get that you'll be fine. Just bridge the two bottom strings with your index. Practice making the changes and switching between chords and you'll get it. When you figure it out call me and we can play."

4

I asked Bill if I could borrow his truck the next weekend to take into town and because he could tell how excited I had become he loaned me the Aston Martin instead. He told me his truck was no vehicle for a lady.

On the way to town I had a clearer purpose, a more defined goal. For the first time since Lincoln I began to feel directed. Driving to her house I passed two coyotes standing on the side of the road, their eyes glinting in my headlights.

Maribel lived on the hill in town, mostly nice houses in the neighborhood. We had just finished working on a song and I couldn't figure out the rhythm.

I said something hurtful that stung her and she withdrew. She set her guitar on her stand then took mine from me and twisted the bottom E string knob until the silver wire snapped. Then she handed it back.

"Now you'll get to learn how to re-string it for the first time," she changed her face into a smile. "C'mon," she stood up. "I want to show you something."

I followed her out of her house and into her white, mid-size truck. We drove away and out of town onto a dirt road, making a small cloud of dust.

The yard we pulled into was overgrown with weeds. I couldn't see the house at first for the trees. Neither one of us spoke as she drove slow.

Up ahead on the path the trees retreated and a small, flat-roofed stone house lay on a short hill. Maribel drove up to the front and parked right next to the front steps. Off to the right was a yellow construction crane and a tan colored pick-up with a seal on its door.

She got out and I followed her. We walked over to the side and she slid up a window. I followed her in.

Still not speaking since leaving the house, we went inside and into the kitchen. We walked through it into the living room. Some moonlight leaked through and made everything bluish gray. We could see black shapes against the dark background. There was no furniture, but Maribel stopped under a six-candle light fixture and turned then walked toward me.

She looked down as we hugged, pressing her face into the center of my chest, and I squeezed my arms around her until I thought I might be hurting her, though she was squeezing back just as hard. Then she pulled her head up and looked at me. It was a soft face, with a trace of a smile in her eyes. Before she could talk and change the feeling of everything I closed my mouth onto hers, holding all of our energy together.

We moved around a little bit but kept our feet in the same place until she took her hands from my hips and took my hand. With the other she put her finger to her lips then led me upstairs.

Up in the bedroom she went to a box in a corner and opened it. I stood by the door and as she walked toward me she smiled and held her palms up. When I took them she put one arm around my shoulder and we held one each in the air, but only for a half of a turn or something. I stepped on her foot and she laughed.

She went over to the corner and shut the box then walked ahead of me, out of the room, down the stairs, then to the window and out to the truck. When we got in she turned on the radio. We were driving back to her house and I thought she was taking me to my car and then the night would be over.

"Let's go back," I said.

She looked at me. Then she stopped on the road and we turned around. We went then with the thickening bond making conversation more difficult. But she was better at these things than I was and smiled.

"Kissed me in the abandoned house. I like it," she said.

We were at the house but before we got out she leaned over and put her hand on my knee. After a second we got out and went to the window. Maribel went in nimble then offered me her hand. I didn't let go as we walked into the main living room. She took my other hand and pulled my arms around her waist with her eyes wide and white, a pure feeling pouring out. She still looked at me with that warmth, that affection.

"Did I tell you? I found this painting of my Granddad's that he made before he died," I said. "And it changes color. I think it changes depending on the color of a person's soul."

"What, like an aura? Are you a hippie?"

"It's kind of like that. Though I don't know if I believe in any of that. Anyway, it's weird, this painting somehow reflects the color of the person who is looking at it."

"That makes no sense. Let's go see it."

"We can't go now. We have to go when no one else is there."

Bill taught me the value of foresight, the value of looking at what you might become if you're not smart enough to appreciate things. Though much of what I saw in him made me sad—the regret and loneliness—he was a wise old man. I told myself while we worked together that I'd be lucky if I possessed half as much knowledge and humor at his time in life. I'd be lucky if I was alive as long as him.

He trusted me more as we grew closer, and the work was good. Every night I went home tired and relaxed. My parents adjusted to the idea of us all living together, their son being at home not long after leaving, and they even showed small signs of pride that Bill and I worked in a smooth way. Mom made more than one comment about our strengthening relationship. When we started, they expected our success to be temporary, but we all enjoyed it when it lasted.

Once the days grew routine with Bill my thoughts remained on Maribel most of the time I was awake. He liked to make fun of me for spacing out in the middle of conversation with the hint of a faraway smile.

"What are you thinking about, son?"

"Nothing. Sorry."

"Don't sorry me, boy, I know who you're daydreaming about. You've got girls on the brain."

I was still having dreams about my impending death, but sometimes I dreamt about her. Those days I woke up and wished I could sleep forever. She called every day to ask me how I wanted to spend our weekends, if we could do this more.

The next time we got together was for her friend's sister's wedding. Weddings are my last and least favorite place, too forced and contrived, but I was trying everything to escape our house and my parents would go along with me going into town to go to a wedding. They were starting to like Maribel. She was smart enough to try and converse with Mom or Dad, whomever she got on the phone whenever she called, and won them over from the beginning.

To get in proper wedding form, I put on a blue suede sport coat I found in my father's closet then drove to town. By then Bill's ancient Aston Martin was basically mine—I drove it home from work everyday rather than making him drive—and he let me have my way with it. The air was cold enough to make me shake as I drove away from the lake, my hands aching as they gripped the steering wheel. Thoughts of Maribel swam behind my eyes, the right way to handle her, the good things to say, how to keep her. This, her, was the only thing I knew I needed to be happy.

At her house she waited by the door and when I knocked she opened it. The dress she wore, blue and black, matched my tie.

We drove in a light mood to the convention hall where they held the reception. Maribel had been invited to the ceremony but

I couldn't ditch Bill in time so she waited for me. There was so much about her I loved, wanted.

I held the door for her as we walked in. In front of us a bar, a guest book, a reception line, and a gift attendant. Maribel handed her a card and we signed the guest book.

That's how it happened with me, I would become more attached by every passing moment, with all of them, until the person who pulled me in the entire time saw how close their rope brought me and when they saw it, because I allowed the gap to narrow without resistance or restraint, they were always surprised. Once she, in the general sense, recognized how enamored I had become, she executed one of two behavior assessments: she either accepted my unearned affection or she rejected my eager suffocation. It all depended on her.

Maybe it was because I was so weak for so long but I thought just saying I would stand next to a girl forever was enough. She told me once to never try and take ownership of her, that she was not mine to have, only to stand next to, but my longing deepened with every act and moment.

Maribel and I went around to the people we knew, her talking mostly and me shaking hands when I knew the men, until we found chairs around a table in the back. We sat down next to a couple who were friends of my parents.

"Carrick," Karen said. "Cheryl said you were home. Back from college?" she smiled and left it there for me. "This is a beautiful wedding. So how long have you two, are you serious, I mean I shouldn't but you've got to get before the chickens. I don't know, I'm drunk."

"Oh nonsense," Maribel said. "You're just warming up. Carrick and I were about to go dancing. I'm going to teach this boy a few moves."

She knew how to swing dance with the grace of a ballerina. She took my hand but smiled before she pulled, asking, and I stood. Knowing enough to know I could only answer one way, I followed her out to the middle of the floor. We entered a dance floor of older couples, the red and blue lights of a DJ, and country music.

The woman who took my hand could not have been more confident and assured. She wanted nothing but to convince me I could relax out in the middle of all those staring dead people. Around us, in the seats at the tables, I imagined faces withering and sinking, the skin tightening to reveal the smooth shape of bones, the flesh falling away. Maribel put her hand on my neck and gave me an encouraging look.

We spun with bent then extended elbows in and out and around in circles. When the merry-go-round spins too fast the kids fly off. She was so strong and graceful that I couldn't have made us look awkward without falling down.

She wove her fingers into mine. She raised our hands up by our faces, looking into my eyes, our arms forming the frames around our faces while we spun. She looked at me with an amused expression; I sported a huge grin pushing out the corners of my face. Despite my embarrassment I was keeping time, grinning like I discovered the answer to everything. With intelligence, she pulled us out of that pose after a few more steps and the song ended.

I untangled my fingers from hers in a sudden and clumsy action. Her face changed from joy to analysis. My embarrassment was moving to a different emotion—I couldn't take her scrutiny. I looked down at the white tile changing to red and blue from the DJ's light. She took my hands into hers to keep me from retreating any farther.

We walked out through the reception area then through the hallway to the parking lot. Cars were lined up and a lighted marquee announced the names of the wedding couple. To our left a friend of my father's stood next to a pillar smoking a cigar. He smiled when he saw us and waved us over.

"Carrick, what happened son? Shit, I could say it was for the best but what the hell do I know? Could be you would make a good doctor. But what do I know? Who's that you got with you there?"

"This is Maribel."

"Maribel. Do you still live here too?"

"Never left."

"Smart that way too. All those other places are just full of people. More people, less space. You can keep all that. Shoot, I'll leave you two alone. Got me some dancin' to do. Saw you two out there. She's a good one."

He walked toward the door.

"Are you sure you don't want to go dance with him?" I said. "I think he liked you."

"Thought about it. But I'd wear him out."

We lucked out and got some warm weather for a few days that November. She was house-sitting for her aunt and uncle who lived a few miles outside of Scottsbluff on a ranch of four hundred acres. It was a nice place, her lawyer uncle settled some of the bigger personal injury suits in the region. The house had been designed by an architect who designed plans for building most of the house underground. Aside from the massive ranch house her aunt and uncle also kept a stable with three horses.

It was night when I drove up in the Aston and Maribel was sitting on the wraparound deck, smoking. She stood up, walked over and met me at the top of the steps. She wrapped her arms around my neck and I rose up to kiss her.

"I like you," she said.

"Let's take out the horses," I said.

"It's freezing."

"We've got coats."

All three of the horses were up when we went in the stable and we could see their breath in the air. I went to the black horse with a white blaze face like a lightning bolt. Maribel laughed and went to the tack box and took out two bridles. I felt Storm's nose with the back of my hand, pressing lightly against the softness. The mare nuzzled me back. Maribel came over and slipped the bit into her mouth and strapped the bridle around the horse's head. She shook the bridle once. Maribel handed me the leather reins.

The saddles and blankets were on sawhorses at the end of the stable. She picked one up with a hand on the saddle horn and one on the back-end and carried it over.

I unlatched then opened the gate. Maribel walked in and threw the blanket and saddle over, buckling the straps under Storm's belly. Then she went to the paint and saddled her.

We took them out, moving slowly. It was almost midnight and the air was cold but we wore sweaters, coats, hats and gloves. We stopped at the beginning of the pasture. I watched Maribel put her foot in the stirrup and mount. She barely touched the saddle horn.

I slid my left shoe into the stirrup and stood, swinging my right foot over. The horse shifted underneath me and I felt the saddle coming over on my left side. But once I swung my right foot into the stirrup I made it. I was on. The stars seemed closer that night, bright and clear, spaced out. Maribel led me across the pasture, following the fence. The movement of the horse was strange as it shifted to navigate the terrain, but after the rhythm became familiar, after I adjusted and moved with her, it felt good.

I spurred Storm as much as felt right with two kicks from my sneakers, but she didn't move.

"You have to let out the reins. She's a good horse. Just let her out a little and have some faith. Heel her a little and hold on with your legs. She'll go."

I leaned forward in the saddle and let out the reins then kicked her again. This time she sped up, bouncing me up on the saddle with a quicker stride. We circled the horses around the pasture fence under the cold winter sky.

5

My parents hired my cousin Tucker to watch me like a child. Mom's work conference was in Los Angeles and they both decided to go to Palm Springs for a weekend. It was November and I didn't resent them for going somewhere warm, just for paying my jackass cousin to babysit. I was nineteen. Yet, after Lincoln, they weren't taking any chances.

I could have gone with them but Bill was hauling cattle and needed my help. For most of the week I just helped Bill during the day and avoided my violent, drunk cousin—shared genetics were the only thing we had in common—until the end of the week.

On Friday he came home from his job at the parts store and started taking off his shirt in the living room.

"I can't stay home and attend to your every need tonight cuz," Tucker said. "There's a poker tourn'ment at the Golden Spur t'night and I'm feelin' lucky."

He went out to his truck and revved it up before throwing rocks as he left the yard. I picked up the phone.

That whole week prior Bill and I worked hard to get his cattle moved to stalks. He owned a twelve-foot trailer and with a hundred head that meant we made a lot of trips. Not that riding in the truck is all that hard, but still I was tired and after I got off the phone with Maribel I sat down in the chair and fell asleep.

I woke up with her sitting on my lap. I've woken up worse ways. She went over and put the movie in and we moved to the couch. We didn't watch past the airplane engine landing on the house. When the credits were rolling I reached to the side and turned off the TV.

"Show it to me," she said.

"It's dark."

"I know. Show it to me anyway. I'm not kissing you anymore until you show it to me. Serious."

There was no way out of that. So I got up and took our coats and a flashlight out of the closet. We walked out across the yard—the moon high above and halved, the air silent. We didn't speak until we came to the shed.

The door of the shed slid open and we went in. I pulled the string for the light and went over to the trunk, but it was still dark so I handed the flashlight to her. She pushed the button, spreading a circle of white on my hands and the latch of the trunk. I opened the lid. The painting was at the bottom, under Grandmother, the hawk, and the pheasant, where I had found it the first time.

I moved the rest of them around, taking two more out. I lifted it from the trunk with the colors facing away from us. I backed up slowly and set it down at our feet. She read out loud the words my Granddad had written.

"The first time I saw this the colors were black and purple, then they changed to purple and blue, then purple and red."

She clasped my waist and stuck her head through, under my arm. I turned the painting around and she shone the light on it.

"That's so beautiful," she said. "That's us."

When she left that night I went back in the house with the colors of my Grandfather's painting covering everything. I felt it then, I was understanding. I believed in love. I believed there was something that would make it possible to stand next to another person for the length of life. There must be. I loved her and I had to find a way to make her know how much I needed her. How much I wanted the thoughts of her to keep me moving forward. She was inertia, motion, the reason for waking.

What to give her? I thought about a locket but I had no picture of us and my mind moved past a gold heart-shaped necklace. I thought about a poem, an attempt at a sonnet with no real craft then went on, thinking about flowers, yellow and white, friendship and passion, but they were missing what I wanted to tell her. LOVE. So I kept thinking. I thought about all the hearts surrounding initials carved in trees, bended knees, ring boxes opening to a shared smile. I thought about all these trite expressions and I waited for a better one to come.

It had to be original. It had to be good. There was something I could do, something with thought and meaning. I knew what she liked and I could use it somehow. I opened up a dialogue with myself. What does she want? A good life, but that has to come from everything, I couldn't just give that to her. What does she like? What does she want from me? Courage, action, music. But how do I use that? Don't make it like you're trying to talk her into something. Give her something good. You're convincing her that you're worth it. That she can trust you. But isn't that boring? Unoriginal? Isn't trust also a symptom of predictability? Yes, in part, but if you want someone to walk across intersections with, that person needs to know you'll watch your side. That you'll be where she expects you. You can surprise her, like what you're doing, or trying to do, now, but she needs to trust you and expect certain things of you before she'll enjoy the surprise. So do this, but don't change yourself so much she feels like she won't know you.

They say if you love something it should be everyone's. I still had the doll from the fountain in Lincoln, but that had no meaning for her, or really, for me. I wanted to give her the painting but I wasn't sure if it was mine to give away. If I was a girl I would give her a lock of my black hair tied in a ribbon, placed in a book of poems. That would be something good. I thought about writing her a song but I wasn't any good, and I knew it was the thought and all, but it had to be good. Enough to express what I felt for her.

My thoughts and feelings were Maribel. She was all. Maribel.

I was enamored with the shape of her, the thought of her. Her. I thought about the biggest, grandest thing I could think of, an enormous body of water. And then, thinking about our conversation in the record store, I knew what it was—the ocean. We would go west until the land ran out and the bottoms of our jeans were soaked in saltwater. I would have to save everything and fix up the Aston for sale, but if I told Bill my plan I thought he would go along with it. He knew how much she was to me.

The next day I woke up with the sun blocked by gray and low humming wind pushing against the walls. It felt good to have a plan and a way to say what I needed Maribel to know. I knew he had been up for hours when I lifted the telephone receiver and called Bill.

"Hi, Bill. Did I wake you up?"

"Heck no, no, not at all. I'm just re-organizing my toy tractor collection. You need to see it. It's looking pretty fancy."

I ate a bowl of cereal then drove to Bill's. The drive seemed to take an instant for all my optimism and happiness, and soon I was at his door, knocking. I heard his voice from deep within the house.

The stale smell of a man living long without a woman rose up as I opened the door. I walked to the den past stacks of unopened mail and over a kid's steel pedal tractor in the living room. I stood at the top of the stairs and saw him bending over to set a green and yellow combine at the bottom of a wooden cabinet in the center of the room.

"You know, and I've been meaning to tell you, I think this is the happiest I've seen you," Bill said. "You're feeling better aren't you? Something to be said for a few days of hard work."

He stopped with the tractors, straightened up, and looked at me. He smiled then went back to the tractors.

Bill's tractor collection ranged down through the history of motorized agriculture. I think he had every type of tractor: John

Deere, Case, International, Massey Ferguson, Allis Chalmers, Hesston, Minneapolis Moline, Oliver, Big Budd, Farmall IH, Ford, David Brown, White, McCormick...everything, and they covered one entire wall of his den. I guess people never stop wanting toys.

"I wanted to ask you something, and I'm sure you'll say no, which you have every right to, but, and I know you've witnessed evidence of this, I'm serious about that what-you-call-pretty lady of mine. The only thing is that I'm not sure she knows that. So... so I'm going to lay it out there. I thought I might fix up the car to sell it so I can do something for her."

He slowed down with his reorganizing and I knew he was thinking.

"You want to sell my Aston Martin?"

As I stood there I realized it wouldn't work. Bill didn't believe in love, he had never experienced it, or at least not the lasting kind, and there was not any way he would think it could work for me.

"Can't do it."

"I thought you would say that. That's fine."

"Nope," he stood again and faced me. "I like that car too much."

"Right. I understand. It's cool."

"And I like you coming over to help too much. Y'see, if I want you to come over and help out, and I do, then I need you to be able to drive over here. If you don't have a car then I don't have any help. And I like you coming around, Carrick. What'd you have in mind? With your lady friend. What'd you have in mind?"

"Well I just thought I wanted to take her somewhere. Someplace good."

He turned back to his tractors.

"All right then. I'll see you later, Bill."

"Wait. Bring my checkbook from the desk upstairs."

He pointed to the other end of the house.

"But you have to promise me that you'll come back. I don't

care that much about the car, but I kind of like having you around. Bring me a check, I'll sign it, and you can write it for whatever you need. But you'll have to work it off. And you have to come back. And tell me all about it."

"Are you sure?"

"It's in the center drawer."

"You don't know how much this means to me."

6

America's farmland spread out like a handmade quilt. From the window of the airliner I saw thousands of my Grandfather's paintings. Most of them were brown and yellow, but some of the alfalfa fields next to the cornfields were our color. When I had asked her, Maribel said yes without hesitation. She asked where I got the money and I told her about the deal I made with Bill. She made me tell her the story twice. It was dark as we came down over Encinitas and the constellation lights of the city glowed up to us.

The airport was empty. We walked down the escalator to the baggage claim. Our bags were the first two out of the carousel, and we took them to the street to hail a taxi.

We asked our driver to take us to a hotel by the beach, somewhere clean and not crowded. He drove us north up the coast on an empty freeway and we looked to our left out the window for the twenty minutes it took to get where we were going.

As we exited west I could see the lights from a lifeguard tower lighting up white water from breaking black waves. We drove into a small coastal district with two blocks of storefronts, restaurants, and bars. It reminded me of old downtown Scottsbluff before the supercenter and the drought started the slow death of closed signs and boarded-up windows.

The taxi took us to a condominium complex of six vacation rentals surrounding a courtyard on a bluff overlooking the ocean. We paid the man and took our bags to the landlady's apartment. She answered in a robe, a big woman with a large face. Then she took us to the corner apartment closest to the ocean and I paid her for the three nights.

We set our bags inside the door then closed and locked it.

"I can smell it," Maribel said. "I love that sound."

We walked to the beginning of a wooden staircase that led down the bluff face. The moonlight reflected off the surface of the black water in a tapered white stripe. A man lay covered in blankets on a bench next to us.

We walked down the wooden stairs to the sand. I stopped at the foot of the beach and took my canvas shoes off and she stepped out of her sandals. I set my shoes next to hers. We rolled up our jeans as we walked, feeling the sand on the bottoms of our feet become more smooth as we walked closer from where the tide had washed away the top layer of sand. A wind swell pushed the waves up and higher than our heads in long breaking lines that shook the beach when they curled over and fell on the sand.

As we walked into the water, we misjudged the timing of the waves and the water came up past our knees, soaking through our jeans.

She held my waist with one arm and I held her by her shoulders, the water rising and falling around our legs.

On the way back we stopped at the top of the stairs and looked across the water. The man in the blankets rolled over but did not wake up. The moon had moved lower in the sky.

At our room I took our bags upstairs and into the bedroom. I slid open the window and the ebb and flow of the waves came back with its calming sound. I was letting the blinds down when Maribel shut our door; the lights were still on and the room was bright as she began to take off her clothes, squared up to me. The slow rush of the waves breaking, rising and falling. I turned and looked at her standing there honest, with courage. She stepped out of her jeans—her hair black, her skin white.

When I awoke I kissed her eyelid. There was a trace of a smile but she remained asleep and I watched her dream. It made me happy to see her sleep and I tried not to make any noise as I took my clothes from the suitcase and found the shower. But I was noisy enough getting in the shower and after the water warmed up she found me rinsing the soap from my hair.

"Let's save water," she said.

We were past needing coffee, awake and clean, when we walked out to the edge of our place to look out across the ocean. It was a clear and cool morning, calm, and I could feel it would be warm in the afternoon. We watched the pelicans float in formation, rising and falling as they flew across the crests of the waves. The swell had relaxed in the night and the surfers were out on the waist-high waves. They were black spots in the water as they sat on their boards in the lineup, waiting for rides into shore.

One surfer caught a chest high wave breaking in a clean right and he was up on the back of his shortboard with a few short paddle strokes. We watched him working to maintain speed, cutting down the wall of the wave, what they called the face, then coming back to the edge of the white water where it was breaking. He would hold his arms out to the side and twist his torso to spray the white water with the tail of his board on his cutback, then drop down the face, only to rise again. Behind the surfers, far out on the horizon, a spout of water rose up in a tiny geyser. A whale was blowing.

We left the lookout, walking under the palm trees lining the street. Ahead, we saw a café on the corner with tables out on the sidewalk. A rastafarian with cropped dreadlocks sat on the bench next to the restaurant playing an acoustic guitar and singing reggae covers. We took a little table under an umbrella and ordered anything we wanted. It was enough to be breathing in sunlight but better because I was now fully in love with Maribel. The food came out fresh and light and we drank organic iced tea while we ate.

"I haven't told you but I applied to school at the community college in Omaha. I should know sometime in the next few weeks. If I get in...well, I don't want to think about it now," she said. "I would have to move, and it's five hundred miles away. I would be pretty far from you."

"I'd just go with you."

With that she stood up and pushed her chair back, catching her thigh against the edge of the table, rattling the plates and glasses. I knew then that I was deeper into the relationship than she was.

She came back and set her water on the table.

"Can we slow down?" she asked.

"Okay."

I didn't understand. Not yet. But I figured if I mulled it over long enough I would.

We spent the rest of the afternoon as super tourists. We took a ferry ride across the harbor and after the ferry we hailed a cab to an art museum. On the cab ride back to our apartment we talked about the paintings and being out on the water as we cruised down the coast. We were tired but happy from the day and we could see the beginning of the sunset on the horizon—the sun falling into the ocean.

Maribel grabbed a bag from the apartment and we stuffed it with a blanket and our hooded sweatshirts. She held my hand as we walked down the wooden steps to the beach, not talking, not wanting to ruin anything. I watched her spread the blanket on the sand and she sat down and smiled at me. We rolled our sweatshirts into pillows and watched the sunset until we fell asleep.

She woke me up by pulling my sweatshirt gently from under my head.

"Look at all of them," she whispered.

Down the length of the beach, as far as we could see, small silver fish were sprinkled on the sand. They sparkled up to the edge of the water and as far back as the tide had risen, nearly up to our blanket. The grunion were about four inches long and glittering, reflecting the moonlight. Maribel reached into the back of my shirt with a cool hand, pressing her body against mine. In a few touches we moved to the blanket.

After we put our clothes back on we folded up the blanket and went down the beach toward the steps, careful not to step on the fish as they wriggled on the sand. At the foot of the stairs we came upon two teenagers kissing.

7

After California we went through the open empty streets of our town like stacked blocks of vivid color. The unrelenting feeling of hopelessness pushed out by our promise for one another. We were heroes, elevated, stronger than any desolate wind humming a low sound across the side of a house at dusk; we were the sound of the past and the future. Of everything and nothing. We could feel the wind. It was at our backs—the sunlight warm on the road ahead.

Then, out of our periphery, a holiday blindsided us and all of my friends were in town for a long weekend. Nate called and said there was a party at Jake's and I told him I'd bring Maribel.

That night she opened the door and her black hair poured into a black shirt, a gold belt wrapped around her waist, a skirt and black knee-high boots. There was no way of knowing what type of foolish things I would say or do in the presence of someone so perfect.

At Jake's house we walked in and she put her hand up the back of my shirt. Her hands were the right amount of soft and warm. Across the living room a record spun and we split off, understanding that as we went around the house with other people, talking and laughing, moving objects with our hands, that each action increased the energy we would apply when we would meet in another room in another part of the house. I watched her, she watched me, and when we caught eyes we stared expressionless, not blinking, testing resolve, driving it up against the wall.

Once I caught her standing in the kitchen with a knife in one hand, smiling, alone. I walked out of the living room, away from her and into the hall and then into Jake's sister's old room and waited with lights on and the door cracked, sitting on the bed with a line ready.

"This is where I take out the photo album and ask you if you want to look at some pictures, you sit next to me, then I seduce you. That is, once you put the knife down."

It might have worked. But she didn't follow, so I turned off the light and walked out. I pirouetted through the house filled with people, turning around to face someone only to turn around again, always changing my tone, changing my stance. Not getting caught, constantly spinning.

We met again under the stairs to the basement.

"Now, listen," she said. "No funny business."

She led me into Jake's gun and trophy room. Showcases of rifles, shotguns, and pistols. Metal on every inch of wall space. At the end opposite the door was a glass case of fifty vertical rifles. But what concerned us was the picture of a cannon that had been dyed into the pattern on the floor rug. I followed her body down as I dropped to my knees, helping with her clothes, and her with mine. I liked the boots and the skirt so they stayed on, and I moved the cotton to the side and she took me out, and before we were in the middle of everything I looked up, around us, to see all the guns on the wall, and just as my eyes made it around the room Maribel shifted to helped make it happen.

After the storm, we reclothed with laughter and shared smiles. I stood and walked to the case at the end of the room and took out a rifle with a short barrel and a long scope.

"You want to help me reload my rifle?"

She didn't laugh so I returned the gun to its case and joined her on the cannon-rug, staring up at the ceiling.

"Can I now safely say that you are mine?" I asked.

"Really?"

"Yep."

"Really, Carrick?"

"Maribel Carter is all mine."

She sat up to look at the guns then she put her head down and re-hooked her bra and took a deep breath.

"Okay, part of it is how you put everything."

"How I put everything?"

"Look. I've told you before. About possession. I don't deal well with that. I'm not yours. Or anyone's."

"That's fine," I said, turning angry. "We'll just take it easy. We'll just take it nice and easy."

"It's nothing about you, Carrick. Don't get upset. You're great. It's me."

I gave a mirthless laugh and moved away. She left. I still sat with my arms around my legs. Strength is nothing in the wake of a good woman who has picked you apart, then put you together, and then turned away.

8

Styrofoam white humps of drifted snow reflected sunlight through the car window on our way to town. They looked plastic, fake, and they would be gone by the end of the day. At the office Mom went in with me and we sat silent in the waiting room. From the table, frozen eyes of celebrities followed the patients around the room.

We hadn't talked for days. I couldn't get myself to call her and I guess she was too afraid of what I might say. That depressed me—to have something I wanted so close, then to watch it walk out of a room and be gone for good. I feigned illness at first. "*I don't know, I don't feel good. I don't know, I feel terrible*."

Mom was smart. She could tell I wasn't physically sick and that it was Maribel, who hadn't called and stopped coming over, and she also knew that I was damaged from Lincoln and now from this.

Kennard's assistant directed me to a chair. A large bald man with glasses and a goatee behind the desk stood and we shook hands. His was an eager, meaty hand.

"Please sit down, Carrick. I'm Dr. Kennard. Call me Bram." He waited for me to sit then slid a notepad off his desk and sat it on his thigh. "How're you doing today?"

"Marvelous."

"Sarcasm. All right, good. Let's start. I'll tell you a little about me. I've been a psychologist for 20 years. Started working in this field after I received treatment for substance abuse addiction. Alcohol, drugs, you name it. Decided that the best way for me to make my peace with all the people I hurt was to help others like me. I've been clean and sober for twenty-two years. Ever use drugs or alcohol? What's your drug of choice?"

"I drink. Sometimes."

"I'm sure a kid your age, shows here you're 19, has a few beers with his friends on the weekend. When I was your age alcohol was long past my drug of choice. By 19 I was in the Army, in Southeast Asia, shooting intravenous whatever-you-could-give-me. But let's talk more about you. Why are you here?"

"My mom wanted me here."

"Why would she want you here?"

"Probably for a number of reasons."

"Specifically. There was a trigger. Something you did or didn't do, something you said."

"It's not that I'm all that depressed, I mean I've had these things happen, not the college part, but it's not like... that's not it, that's not what I mean. There's more than that ...you know what? I don't know what I'm thinking and I don't know why I'm here."

"Carrick, your attitude and tone change signals to me there's something underlying there. When you change to defensive mode that's when I become concerned. I know we've just met but if this is going to work for you then you're going to have to trust me when I say only by talking about this can you hope to reach any understanding."

"Right. I know how this is supposed to work. Sorry if I can't accurately explain the inner workings of something as simple as my brain. So...I'm supposed to talk to you until we dig up everything, look at it, then by shedding light, or whatever, as if you're all-wise and all-knowing, we'll reach this so-called understanding and I'll walk out of here empowered and enlightened. Is that pretty close?"

"That's not how I would put it exactly. That might be a little too much to hope for. But your assessment of the process is close to correct. Let me ask you this. Was it because of something that happened to you recently?"

"Can I ask you how much you get paid to ask these questions?"

"Not now. Let's stay on track. Was it something that happened to you recently?"

"I don't have health insurance."

"Can we get back to you and...see, to me, it seems you are depressed. Are you religious? Do you pray or go to church?"

"I don't have any faith in any of that. Most of the people I know who go to church are unable to cope within their own means. It all seems like superstition to me."

"You know, that's funny, because when I was in my early twenties, shooting up a thumb's worth of horse at a time, I believed close to the same thing. But after time, and seeing patients go from sick to healthy and back again, religion and prayer is good for those lonely people, those with anxiety and depression. Can you see how that would work?"

"It's just that really, my main concern, the thing that I'm obsessed with, that confuses me, that bothers me, that I won't let go, I can't define...I can't describe or articulate."

"Try."

"Okay, here: There's a voice on the phone saying things I can't hear; there's a character on my television with no face; there's a green sign I pass on my way to work with white words I can't read; there's a book on my shelf written in my handwriting but in a language I can't understand."

"Well...that doesn't really help. Try relating in terms I can understand. Tell me how it feels."

"It makes me sad. It makes me angry. It makes me confused. It makes me want to sleep. It makes me say words that are supposed to convey my emotions."

"Why would you want to sleep? Are you physically tired?"

"No."

"What do you want?"

"Right now? To go home. To get out of this office."

"No, what do you *really* want?"

"What do you want?"

"This is about you. But I'll tell you. I want to be happy, to have a good job and a little money."

"How is your job or money going to make you happy?"

"I didn't say it would. I said I wanted those things. They're separate."

"But having a job and money will make you happy."

"No. That's not how I see it. You can be happy without those things."

"So...what you want and what makes you happy are different?"

"That's enough about me. I asked you a question Carrick, and you still haven't answered it. What do you want?"

"I don't know. I guess I don't want to say everything I imagine, walking around asking people meaningless questions, holding out for money...I guess...sometimes there's a viewpoint that makes everything the most clear, provides the most clarity."

"I was a lot like you once, Carrick. Unwilling to accept anything as right for me, constantly looking, not sure this way or that way was right or wrong. I was always looking for something different than what I had, never willing to accept anyone's opinion, argumentative, constantly questioning. And I'm not saying it's bad to question, but you'd be much happier, things would be much easier, if you would just surrender. Accept things as they are. Go along with it. Surrender. If there's anything I want you to do when you go home it is to try that. Just start by saying yes first. Can you do that?"

"I'm not making any promises. Why are you a psychologist?"

"I like doing this."

"It looks like you're having a blast."

9

Snow refused to fall and the people in the community were talking about dust bowls. Constant wind drug clouds of dust across the blank plains. My skin and lips dried then cracked; my knuckles split open to bleed but clotted and scabbed as fast as they could open. I couldn't make a fist or grip anything tight without my skin ripping apart. The phone rang. It was Maribel. Four knuckles tore open at once on my right hand. I held my hand over the sink. Spreading my fingers apart helped the blood run between my fingers and drip into the white porcelain. I dropped the phone when I realized the hand holding the receiver was bleeding as bad as the right.

No grass grew in Scottsbluff. Pioneer's Park was all dead leaves and brown grass. My black shoes kicked up small puffs of dust as I walked toward her. I had so many things I wanted to tell her, to ask her—I had stayed awake with the lights off thinking about the path our conversation would take. This was my chance to get it off my mind.

She stood leaning against a giant turtle statue looking like a fall tree scene. Her ankles crossing khakis, up to a green sweater and wide black sunglasses blending into her black hair. She rubbed the turtle's shell.

"We're buds," she said, rising from the statue to hug me but there was pain in my response and it didn't come off well. She pointed to a picnic table alone under a brown roof. We sat across from each other at the table and I could feel myself withdrawing the longer I sat there. The wind blew her hair off her shoulders in short bursts. She took my hands.

"You don't look okay," she said.

I looked at our hands then at her black sunglasses. I pushed the hair from my eyes.

She shook her head then removed her sunglasses.

"Look, Carrick. This isn't working. This is hard for me to say, but—"

She stood up. I watched her walk to the sidewalk and down the street until she disappeared behind a building. I fell to my side then turned onto my back and stared up to the sun.

On the drive home, in dust clouds and wind, I thought about all the words I couldn't speak. My mind focused on my inability to say the things I was thinking. How the words I resolved the night before ran through my head at the picnic table, and how I failed to utter any part of them. I wanted to save her from them, or I wanted to save myself from knowing her truth. I thought about how maybe love and truth aren't always good for each other. That truth is the one thing that destroys love, and love the one thing that can hide truth. That you cannot have one with the other. I thought about how little I really knew about love.

As I parked my car in our yard, the wind slowed down but thick clouds came in, covering everything and dimming the light. Mom and Dad were at Grandma's, where they often went after church, and I went into my room and lay on my bed, wrapping the bedspread over my body and over my face. I would have slept with all the serotonin drained from my head, but the more I thought about my failure to speak the more I shook. Through my shoulders and stomach and into my back, my muscles shivered then seized as if they were repeatedly shocked.

When the shaking and the blanket drove my body temperature up to a low fever, I got off my bed for water and to go outside for air. I stared at the carpet down the hallway, at one point sliding my shoulder against the wall for stability. The faucet filled my cup but my stomach hurt from the shivering. A sip but that was it.

After I sat the cup down I looked up through the window. In the time I spent shaking, heavy snow fell in white flakes the size of quarters. It came down with no great speed and watching the silent way it fell muffled everything in my head.

But it wasn't long before the silence within my mind was broken and Maribel and the park returned with sharp clarity and sound. All of it rewound and replayed. I knocked the cup over and sat on the floor with my back against the cupboard. Outside, thick white snow and a darkening gray sky.

The snow fell steady from after the day with Maribel on through Christmas. It covered the ground and rooftops and stuck in the trees. Our phone rang once a night from the start of Christmas break. Mom usually answered and told my friends I couldn't come to the phone. Those were my specifications, but it was fine with her—that way I couldn't get into any trouble.

It surprised me when Nate knocked on our door the day after Christmas. Mom let him in and I was sitting on my bed, pulling the strings out of my guitar, when he came in. I set it down and lay back in my bed.

"Dude. Why don't you put on some clothes and we'll go outside for a walk. You could use the air."

"It's snowing."

"You've been in snow before. It's actually not that bad out. It's still coming down, but the sun's out and it's not that windy. C'mon. I've never seen the lake in the winter."

I stood up then shuffled through my door to the hallway closet. From it I took out a blue cover-all and a white beanie with a blue ball on the top. I put them on over my clothes in the hallway. We walked out of the house into a silent, still landscape. The only sound came from the sparrows in the trees and our boots on the snow. From the edge of our yard the remaining water was far off, a speck of glass in the distance.

The way led us along the edge of the trees, past our neighbors, past all the houses. We walked on the snow where the sand met the woods. So much snow had accumulated in the trees that as we walked we would hear the sound of the branches releasing in small avalanches, the falling snow breaking the silence.

We were in the preserved, undeveloped part of the lake. Our direction took us away from the snow-covered sand into the trees, until there were trees all around and we could see nothing else.

"This is what I wanted to show you."

We came upon a clearing in the trees. At the far end a two-story gray, stone chimney rose up from the ground. We walked to the center of the clearing.

"Do you really believe that?" Nate asked.

"My Dad said this house belonged to a family of this guy and his three daughters. Dad didn't say what he did or where the mother was, he just told me that the family that lived here built the house. I guess it was more made out of logs, like a log cabin. They built it themselves. Dad called it a "life's labor." So, however long ago, when some certain type of bird native to this region became endangered, the state decided to make this area of the lake a state preserve. Which meant no hunting or trapping, no fishing or boating in this section of the lake. But it also meant no residents, to preserve the natural eco-system, it meant no human contact. So, the family was going to be forced out, but they wouldn't leave, fighting in the courts, passing out petitions, and they prolonged the process until a radical environmental organization came out here at night and burned it down. With them in it. All but the youngest daughter died. He said the father carried her out first then went back in, but the walls were made out of these heavy logs and one of them collapsed and the youngest daughter was the only one that made it. We're not the choices we make. We're what the world makes of us. It's freezing. We have hot cider in the house and firewood. Let's go back."

"I don't think I'm going to stay and hang out," Nate said. "I just wanted to stop and see my old friend. Hey, there's a party at Kendra's house on Friday. You should come. You could stand to get out of the house, right?"

"Sure. We'll see. Call me, though. Will you?"

"I'll call you."

10

Nate coming out to visit made me feel more alone. Not that it wasn't good, it was, but after he left my thoughts stuck on him and what he was doing, at college, on this break, seeing all of our friends, going out, having a good time. The snow continued to fall and there was no work to be done at Bill's. It wasn't calving season yet and the cattle were out on stalks, and the only maintenance Bill performed was routine checking and putting in the occasional bale of straw. That he could handle on his own.

Again, Mom sent me to Kennard. After the last visit he told her he needed to see me again before he could diagnose me, but, he said, I might need to be working with a psychiatrist. He told her my depression might be too deep to pull out of without pills.

The ride into town grated. We drove the eight miles slow, on bad roads. Mom wanted to talk.

"I really hope this is helping."

"I think it is."

"Do you like the doctor?"

"No, not really. But he's good enough at what he does."

"What do you guys talk about?"

"The usual psychology stuff. How does that make you feel? What I'm afraid of. Why I can't get out of bed."

"Does he think you're depressed?"

"I'm sure."

"Do you think you're depressed?"

"I think I...I'm...I don't know. I can't really say. Can we just relax? I'm going to be doing plenty of talking when I'm in there with him."

White plains inched by out my window. Ahead of us, two thousand miles down the road, on the coast of California, the ocean lapped at the shores. A lifeguard watched the waves curl over a rock break with perfect shape. Off on the horizon, a battleship sailed toward Asia.

"Sit down Carrick. It's good to see you. How are we feeling today?"

"I don't...it doesn't matter. Are you going to ask me questions?"

"That's on the agenda yes. But if you want, we can start by talking about anything. It's up to you. What have you been doing?"

"Sleeping. Staying up late. Reading."

"Anything else?"

"No. Why does this matter?"

"Okay Carrick, new rule: no more 'why' questions. I'm going to encourage you to express yourself in the form of statements. And try to express your emotions."

"I've been dreaming lately.

"Tell me about your dream."

"Okay it's sort of reoccurring. I think that I've dreamt it three times. It's different each time, I mean it starts different, but ends the same. Somehow I always lose her. I start the dream with her then something happens and then I'm in a tunnel, with something behind me, pushing me down the tunnel, chasing me...until I start to see this orange glow at the end, and in the dream I always think it's the way out, the light, but when I get there, every time, it's an enormous jet engine. It's just parked at the end, a roaring, gaping fire, waiting for me. I don't want to lose her."

"Is this upsetting you?"

"The feeling I get, and I had this feeling before, in Lincoln. It's as if there is a metal band around my head, constricting, squeezing, almost like those halos they use for broken necks, where bolts are drilled into your skull. I imagine what I feel is slightly less severe than that. That I *can* describe. I know what that feels like and the feeling is clear in my head because the sensation is distinct. That is one of them. But the other, this thing more recently, is different.

"Lately, when I was driving with my Mom, actually just the other day, we came up to this bridge over the river, and I've never felt this before this day. All of the sudden I asked her to stop, to pull over, that I couldn't cross the river right there. She didn't hear me right away, I muttered it, and we were getting closer but she wasn't slowing down so I pulled the door handle to open the door but the locks were on. I couldn't speak as we came closer. She kept driving, asking me what was wrong but I couldn't tell her and I was pulling on the door handle and she was getting closer. I wrapped my fist in my coat and as we came over the river I reached for the gearshift but she was fighting me off, asking me what I was doing.

"I still get tense when I think about it now. She kept going and I closed my eyes and we made it across but I was unable to speak for a while. Then I unclenched my fist. So there's the halo, the bridge, and the tunnel. The halo hasn't been tightened for some time, since Lincoln, and we don't cross the river right now. But I can't control my dreams."

"It's a good thing you have those locks."

"I haven't talked to anyone about the halo for a long time."

Until that my mind was wrapped in our conversation, thinking about my responses, my reactions, but then my thoughts reflected on the difference in that talk and the last time I sat in the chair. It wasn't because of Kennard, but for the most part during this session I had spoken with clarity, well enough to accurately convey my thoughts.

"Are we done yet?"

"Almost. Carrick, can you tell me about Lincoln? About what

went wrong in that short time?"

"I could tell you what happened. I remember it. But I couldn't tell you why."

"Do you want to tell me what happened?"

"You'll want to ask me questions about it, and I won't be able to answer them."

"I might be able to help with that."

"No, I don't think you will. Look, my ride's here, and our time's up."

"Okay, think about it. For next time I want you to come in with one thing about why you think what happened in Lincoln did happen as it happened."

"Okay."

"Set up your next appointment with Stacy on your way out."

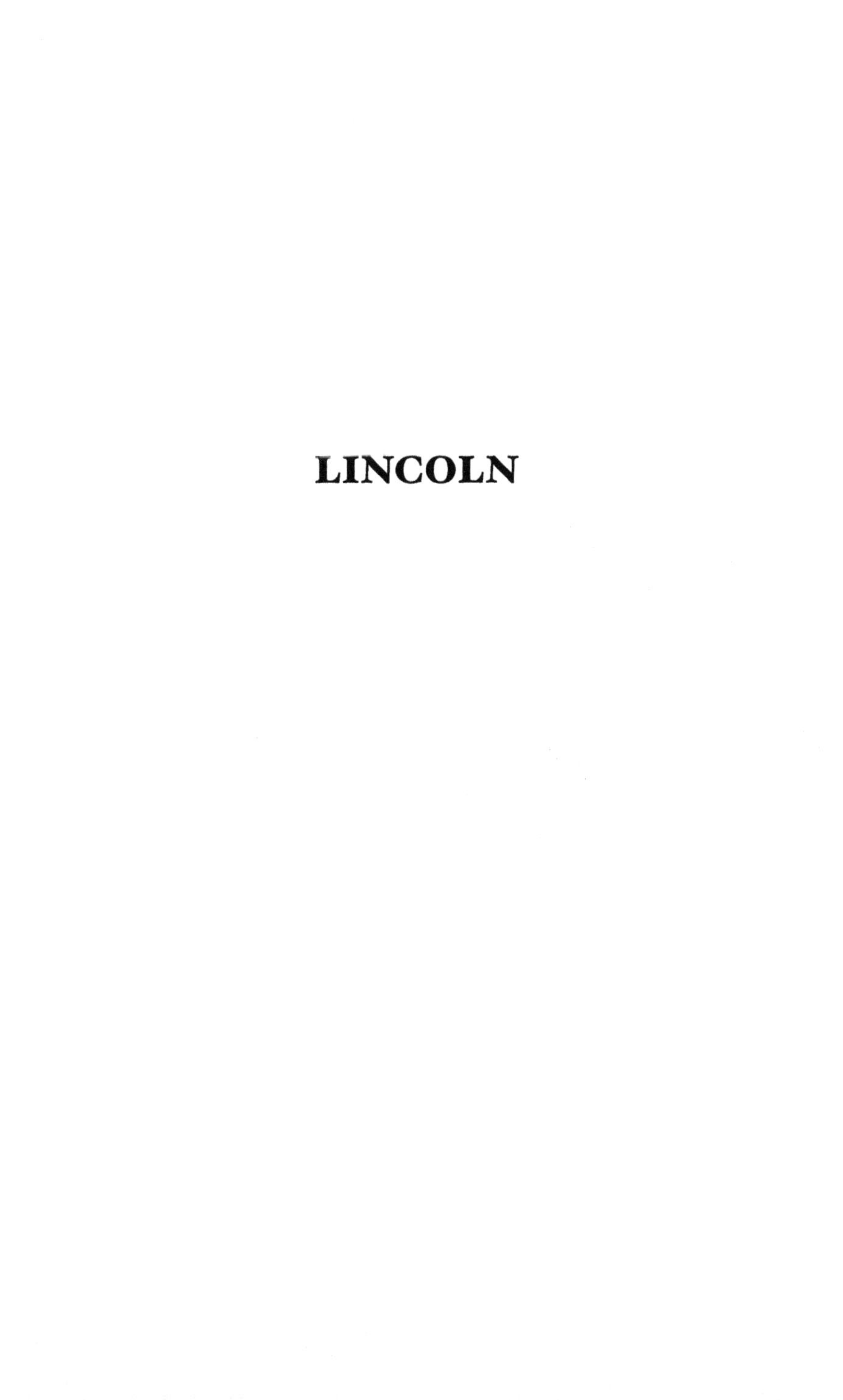

LINCOLN

II

As a challenge to myself, I wanted to answer Dr. Kennard's question. I had no real explanation of why things went as they did when I left for Lincoln. All I could really do was recount what happened and try to make some sense of it. For some reason I'm not sure of, when I left Scottsbluff I became a person I had never been before.

The summer after senior year, before I met Bill and Maribel and Dr. Kennard, when a couple of fraternity guys from Lincoln came recruiting in the middle of July, they didn't have to do much convincing to get me to join. I signed a card then drove across the dried-up corn and wheat fields to the other end of the state in my black, rusted car until I showed up at the parking lot of the fraternity.

Apparently everyone gets to college a week early. That way they can all destroy themselves with alcohol as many times as possible before the first week of classes. I wasn't given that information and showed up the night before school started. When I got up to my room I pulled open the door and the first thing I remember was the smell of vomit. According to my new roommate McPherson, who was sitting on the couch drinking one of last night's beers, our room, the room I was assigned to, was designated the party room. The older guys that did the room deciding must have loved the way I looked wasted when I signed their card in Scottsbluff and wanted to see it over and over every night, all semester.

All week before I showed up there had been trash cans full

of beer and frat boys and sorority girls destroying themselves. Rubbing their bodies against other bodies until the girls got too drunk and left, doing weird shit you don't want to know about. That's what you want to see when you show up at college—beer cans scattered everywhere, a soggy, musty smell in the air and a roommate, Mr. McPherson, who was sitting on our only piece of furniture, a sofa from the 70s, drinking beer on a Sunday afternoon.

"Grab yourself a beer Willy, if you don't mind. We should celebrate your arrival," he said. "I'm McPherson, or Mac, and, Linus, your other roommate went to go find some candles to help cover up the funk. We just threw a wild party—everyone got wrecked. I bet we packed twenty girls from every sorority in here."

After McPherson told me which bed I would be sleeping in I told him I needed to get something out of my car. Then I walked out of the frat house and headed away from campus. I felt bad for showing up after all the fun and could feel the stress of the first part of college coming on.

That night I wasn't sure where I was going. I kind of knew the town—it was the state capital. I had visited earlier in the summer and I knew there was an apartment complex down the road where almost all college kids lived. I did not like being alone, not knowing anyone, but I wasn't complaining. I was alive, in a new place, my parents four hundred miles away, free to do whatever I wanted and walking under a cloudless August sky. The more I thought about it, the more I was in the mood to go out, to find the best party of my life and meet the cutest girl, fall in love and get married. Have the happiest life in the history of the world.

It was getting dark in that slow, creeping, summer night way—dusk moving in and over me in growing degrees of darkening gray, the color leaving everything and being replaced by black, the white and yellow of artificial lights streaking through. It came on fast and I walked past rows of white, immigration-era houses while the streetlights hummed over my head. The small houses all had lawns that bordered the buildings, some with fences, some with dogs that ran after me as I walked. I imagined a girl riding past on a pink bike with white handlebar streamers and a white basket on the front.

As I came up to the apartment complex I could hear the sounds of a party coming toward me. There's always a low bass line that carries out farther than the rest of the noise. The corners of my mouth stretched a little, and I could feel the smile forming in my eyes. I stood there in the middle of the apartment complex for a minute or so, judging the sound, until I decided to head toward an apartment where two girls stood outside smoking. Rad, I thought to myself, with two girls on the railing this was going to work out good.

I walked slowly, my hands in my pockets, but I thought it seemed too casual and lazy, so I took them out and slightly swung my arms. I wanted to be confident, or confident enough to make it seem like I knew where I was going. I kept my head up, looking at the girls. They were laughing but got kind of quiet as I came up the stairs. I watched them without breaking my gaze.

When I got to the top they finished their cigarettes, threw the butts off the balcony and were about to go inside.

"Hey," I said, kind of hopeful, but that didn't slow them down. So I smiled, right, like nice and optimistic. "What's going on out here? I'm Carrick. What's your name?"

I focused on her, she was cute, blonde, and I liked to give one person my undivided attention. Something that works when people do it to me, I guess. It performed the desired effect and the other girl went inside so it was just me and—

"Carmen."

"Hi Carmen. Would you mind having another cigarette out here with me? I just moved here and don't know anyone quite yet."

"Where'd you move here from?"

"Scottsbluff."

"I know someone from Scottsbluff. What's his name?"

I stood there for a second while Carmen looked up to the sky, looking for a name of some guy I didn't like in high school. I wanted her to hurry up so we could start with the falling in love and moving to California, hoping she'd get on with the thinking or take her cigarettes out of her purse. She was killing me. She fumbled around with her bag, rattling all her belongings. This was not how a guy and a girl fall in love, all awkward and rattling and fumbling. She finally took out the lighter, then paused, "it's so close, on the tip of my. I can see his face. He's tall, about your build, but his hair's not nearly as dark."

She gave me the cigarettes after what was at least two years. I took out two and reached for the lighter. Oh no, no fairy tale romance was going to involve her lighting my cigarette. I can be real chivalrous sometimes, and I lit the cigarettes and handed one to her, with a smile.

She went in then and it didn't take long for her to find us two beers, come back, and announce she could only have one more then she needed to go over to her boyfriend's place. They were supposed to go hot tubbing, she said. I wanted to tell her to keep the explanation.

Sweet, Carmen. Real sweet. Go hot tub yourself to death. I turned around and looked over the edge of the balcony, then climbed up on the rail and looked down. I think she might have been worried about me or something; she told me to come down, and when I did she gave me her number—made me put it in my phone before she left. As if I wanted a number of some girl with a boyfriend.

After Carmen bailed I came down from the balcony, walked down the stairs and out of the apartment complex. I could have gone into the party and met some drunken morons but I didn't feel like it. No, instead I took out my class schedule and decided to go find the buildings where I would be going to class.

Before I left for Lincoln, when I was packing up all my belongings, I had looked at my schedule in some cheesy college scene, my suitcases on my bed, my favorite cap on the shelf by the door, Mom waiting for me to give her a hug so she could tell me good luck, wave me off.

I knew I had class at nine-thirty the next morning and since it was getting late by then I thought I'd find my first classroom. All the smart kids were sleeping and I could have gone home and to bed too, but I just got there and that would have been lame.

So I walked out of the apartment complex and over toward the university, feeling bad because of Carmen. I hate that down you feel when you're getting real into one and she's smiling, and you start to think about what's hanging from her rearview mirror, and you're hoping she listens to the same music as you. If I could have stepped into that hot tub with her I could have died right there. That's what girls do to me, a smile, a touch, and I'm shaking and thinking about moving to California, disappearing. She was beautiful, and sometimes, when it's going right, like right before she said that crap about her boyfriend, you start to see yourself sitting next to her and driving out to a park and walking under the stars and maybe even holding hands if you have to, but then you hear something like "I have a boyfriend". Then it's over. You're done. And the sarcasm kicks in and everybody's sweet and you walk away, maybe not even saying bye or nice to meet you.

That's where I was, walking away from the whole Carmen deal toward a dark campus, toward the streetlights of the walkways and the dark buildings. I walked past that giant monument to brains and book learning, the football stadium. The stadium looked like a miniature version of the coliseums of gladiators, a very miniature version, and I thought about how great it would be to be able to carry a sword, or an axe, or any old-fashioned weapon. I thought about some jackass fighting a lion or a tiger with a piece of metal, getting his face mauled off.

I walked past the stone walls and statues of men fondling and rubbing all over other men and I could almost hear the grunts and high fives and people screaming. Screaming because it feels good to scream, not because they really cared about the steroid junkie linebacker who's better at sticking a needle between his toes than algebra.

One thing about the university, they didn't strain any mental muscles to come up with the architecture for the buildings. You'd think with all the intellectual superiority and stimulation inside all those classrooms, all those scientists and thinkers, they could have invented something a little better, a little easier on the eye. Almost all of them were rectangle, brick buildings laid out on their long side. They were all the same size and same red brick color, lined up end to end in an oval around the campus. These guys were real creative. Must have put a lot of effort in drawing out the plans. Oh, I don't know, I think we should put another box just like the last over here, right next to this one. How about this, guys? Let's put a whole row of identical buildings right there. What do you think? Too risky? Guys?

I looked at my schedule and it said my first class was in the Johnson building but I had no idea how to find it from where I was, no idea what direction it was in. Walking away from the stadium, I headed down the twisted sidewalk paths toward the lights of the Union, thinking maybe they had a map. Bushes hedged the sidewalks and the path went up and down in small hills. The lights above the Union lit up the fountain out front and I walked up to it.

Then Carmen.

"Hey, I like you, you're cool, let's drink and smoke cigarettes. I'll flirt with you and smile. But, oh, wait. What's that? Oh, I have a boyfriend. See ya! Too bad!"

Shaped in the form of a geyser, the fountain spilled up and out over small boulders and a pool of water formed a ring around the gray stones. I took off my shoes, put my socks in them, and rolled up my jeans. The stale, lukewarm water felt good on my feet.

As I waded out into the water I saw a blonde doll in a yellow dress floating face down, her arms outstretched above her head. I walked until the water came up around my calves and I was close enough to pick her up. Her yellow dress dripped and the plastic hair kept its shape when I lifted her from the water.

At first I thought I'd put her back since she didn't belong to me. But I couldn't throw her into the pool only to have some maintenance worker fish her out, then toss her in the box of his white pickup in with the weeds and trash. Some girl somewhere loved her, missed her. So I picked her up and put her in the pocket of my black jeans with her face looking forward and plastic blonde hair spilling out. I was happy to have a new friend.

After I left the pool and picked up my shoes, I thought it'd be nice to find a hotel, maybe get some room service. I thought about going to the frat, back to that shithole, but I didn't want to unpack my stuff, smell the puke, talk to McPherson—didn't want to deal with it.

I walked away from the university until I could see a hotel. In that minute I could not think of doing anything else. I didn't have any friends, just the doll. The sidewalks I walked on were empty and if there were any cars they ripped through the silence.

For a while the scene faded from distinct faces and clear lines as I seemed to be moving in shades of formless color. This was when it began. Much of what I waded and swam through was black and yellow, and the way I remember it always comes through in two ways: color and temperature. The fever could have come from any number of things, the doctors think they know but they're just as confused as me.

One thing I do know, I know it was hard to focus enough to even walk. I dropped my shoes on the sidewalk and put them on, leaving my socks in the gutter. Drops of sweat poured out down my face. I gasped with my mouth open and lungs pumping hard. It seemed my eyes could not get any wider and I walked off fast, at a quick, arm-swinging pace. Something started on fire and I needed to get off the street, get anywhere fast. In my pocket, the doll looked on unphased, unblinking, perfectly fine and happy to be in a warm, dry place.

After walking in my sweat and blurred vision, I found a chain hotel. A red smear of a hotel desk clerk checked me in, asking if I was all right. I grunted, then leaned over, and with my hands on my knees I spat out that I needed a room—rocking back and forth, bending my knees, saliva building in the back of my throat. Whatever it was, it took a good hold of me. The clerk said it might be a good idea to get some sleep, that I didn't look too good. I gave him my card, then asked where the elevator was and took the key he handed to me.

In front of the elevator, I sat on the floor, hugging my knees and muttering the room number out loud while I waited for it, fighting collapse. Once inside, the elevator ride tortured me in a claustrophobic suffocation, my heart thudded, and I needed to stand or risk riding it to the top. I pulled myself up. I wrung my hands together during that split second when the elevator stops and the doors hold closed as you wait for the bell and the sound of opening. The splitting of the doors to the hallway and the widening of light seemed somehow similar to what was happening inside my head.

A red line of carpet and white spots of centered ceiling lights stretched down straight away, growing wider as the elevator doors opened. I stumbled from the elevator, walked by sliding my shoulder against the wall, then staggered down the hall until I found my room. The red and yellow lights of the keycard reader lit up, winking at me and increasing my frustration until I knelt in front of the door and swiped the card from my knees. The light turned to green and I pulled down the handle.

When I came in the room I collapsed. It wasn't that I was tired, but the burning behind my forehead made it impossible to stand. I took off my shirt before falling through the opening. My head begun to boil, swell, and fill with concrete as I crawled through the door. The weight of a thousand sidewalks wrapped around my face.

My mind would not give in to the same pressures as my body, and after a few minutes of paralysis, I put my shirt on, stood, staggered, then switched on the TV, closing the curtains and turning the air-conditioner on high. I sat in front of the blowing fan for a long time before I felt any better. It was awful, really, and the fan didn't help much. I left the room dark, the only light coming from the flashing images of the television, and took a corner of the sheets and blankets from the bed, pulled them off, and then, piling them in the corner, I crawled onto the bed.

But my mind didn't want sleep; instead I climbed up and stood on the center of the mattress, watching the television. The springs of the bed balanced my weight as sweat poured into my eyes, down my cheeks, and off my chin. It wasn't until I blanked out staring vacant at the TV that I remembered the doll in my pocket. I took her out and sat her up in front of the alarm clock on the nightstand. Her blue eyes watched the television not unlike I did. When I set her down I saw the phone and dialed zero.

After I placed my order I looked down at my left hand and on it the word "War" was stamped in black block letters. I rubbed it and it smeared into a black slick on the back of my hand. Sweat dripped down my neck and collected in the cotton of my shirt.

Then I thought about Carmen and her number in my phone. She smiled in my imagination, walking down the steps of a hot tub in a bikini as she looked at me. I took the phone out as I stood there on the center of the mattress, thumbing the buttons until I found her name then hit talk. The phone dialed her number as I held it in my hand and I heard her answer with a distorted hello.

She sounded confused so I hit end. My imagination turned and I saw her hugging her boyfriend, sitting on his lap in the hot tub. I stood there in the center of the bed, watching TV until the hotel girl knocked and brought in my room service. She pushed the cart into the room then backed straight out, staring. I would have stared too—I'm sure I looked like a maniac.

Sitting on the windowsill, I ate the two bananas and bowl of chocolate ice cream as I watched the television. It made me feel worse. Around my chest and shoulders my shirt was soaked in sweat, sticking to me. I paced on the carpet, counting in a one-two-three-four pattern as I went back and forth, back and forth, one-two-three-four. Those four numbers the only words I could run through my head without tripping over them, having them trigger guilt or a memory. I watched my feet move as I paced. A semi-truck drove over a ship in a bottle. The TV was on, making noise I could not understand, and I sweated as I paced and the air conditioner blew and I went back and forth, back and forth, one-two-three-four.

12

I stopped pacing when the maid knocked with the towels the next morning. My bare feet were wet and cold against the plastic carpet as I went to the door. She handed me a towel but I didn't let her in, never unchaining the door, and the beep from my pocket meant the battery on my phone was dying. I draped a white towel over my head and went into the bathroom, taking the towel and wiping myself off. After I undressed then put the same soggy clothes back on, I decided I needed to find some new clothes and a new hat. Maybe I could find some friends while I was at it.

I still had not slept when I left the hotel but I wasn't tired in my head. I think the whole sickness-nightmare fueled me with its delusions, taking me up and away from the ground so that I seemed to be hovering around my body, detached and floating in the air.

The burning in my forehead subsided or I didn't notice anymore, but I still sweated a little and my skin was damp. My eyes stung from the sweat they collected. I tried to remember the last time I broke a sweat, the last time I felt so exhausted and alive. I thought to the day in July when Jake and I hiked across the hills behind Scottsbluff in the middle of the afternoon, when we saw a rattlesnake eating a smaller snake, when the sun burned through his glasses to light the brush on fire, when we thought we started a fire to burn the city to the ground, when we were disappointed when it didn't.

My feet hurt from the pacing and I could feel them far away in a dull, unattached aching but they continued to work so I walked on, past a crack in the sidewalk, past a penny I left on the ground, past a blind man's cane, past a trap door to the center of the world.

After walking with my head down in the mid-morning light, I looked up to find I was at a sporting goods store. It seemed as if the store and I came together for some reason. I pulled on the door but I struck my shoulder on it when I went to go inside, so I opened it again and made it through the second time.

Inside, behind a counter in the center, an old man moved in slow, shuffled steps. I stuck my hands in my back pockets and went up to the counter in the middle. Pistols and bullets were encased in glass under the cash register. Rows and rows of silver revolvers, and I thought about the weight and feel of a gun in my hand. Holding the gun with an extended arm.

All around me, the place was stocked with coats and hats, duck calls and goose decoys, and those sad—sadder than the zoo—animal heads on the walls. I wanted to swing from the antlers of the big bull moose above the entrance. The store itself must have taken clothing donations and worked as a half-Salvation Army and half-retail store. In the back were a bunch of old appliances—wooden console televisions and old blenders, boxes of old clothes.

The whole store made me sad. I walked through the store avoiding the eyes of the old man until I got to the boxes. I could not see very far ahead of me, so I sat on the ground and went for the pile of hats in a brown cardboard box on the floor. My thighs ached as I sat cross-legged and I noticed a rattle in my breathing. I sorted through two or three until I found an old hat that looked different than anything I ever saw any of my friends or anyone young wear. It was something only a man in overalls should have, half-mesh, half-foam, and camouflage. The bill was flat and the barn of the hat was ridiculously tall. I took it up to the man at the counter and asked him to hold on to it, setting it on the counter next to the cash register. I looked around some more, finding a shoulder strap backpack I liked.

But the things that interested me most were the kayaks. Standing in front of one, a yellow one, I ran my hands across the fiberglass finish. I liked the hole for one man and the lack of space for anything other than myself. I smiled while I looked at, imagining the rapids I would negotiate and master with my double-sided oar. Not figuring the cost really, I walked over to the counter and told him I would put down a deposit, handing him my credit card. From the stand next to me, I grabbed a backpack and handed it to him before he swiped my card in silence, then I put on the hat he held at the register.

I walked out of the store wearing a camouflage hat, a new backpack, and carrying the receipt for a down payment on a kayak.

Because I was becoming a kayaker, I needed a map or some type of literature to know where to use the thing. I headed over to the public library. The library was a place of comfort; I could always find solace among the stacks of knowledge.

As I entered the building the hotel feeling washed over me, and I sort of forgot what I came there for—it seemed all I could do was stumble around trying not to bump into the tables or knock anything over. The place was empty and the ladies behind the counter seemed occupied with their computers and bar codes. But still a pressure remained. The library air made me want to take off my shirt and lie down on the middle of the floor. My hip banged into a table and I looked up at a librarian who, with glasses at the tip of her nose, looked over them to check on me.

After that I could feel the eyes of the librarians burning into my neck but I held it together long enough to make it upstairs to the literature section. The air seemed thick and heavy up there and I wanted find a window. I didn't care where, I just wanted to escape the eyes of the librarians and find fresh air and sunlight.

The patterns on the shallow carpet reminded me of my house, where I played and sat on the floor. I looked up and found myself surrounded by rows and rows of books with titles I could not read; I would read the first or second word on a spine only to have it enter into my bloodstream, clotting and sticking in my veins until it hit my heart and fluttered the muscle, making me lightheaded. This was sensory suffocation. Somewhere behind a mirrored window a doctor looked at another doctor and shook his head. Up in the stacks of books I spun dizzy circles in slow, defeated rotations—sweating and hoping for an end to the fever.

There really was no chance the literature was going to get me anywhere, but I thought that by pulling anything down from the stack I might find a sentence or a picture to distract my mind. Maybe a book could change my focus long enough to send me on another path.

I pulled down the closest thing I could reach and read a passage dealing with devils in cornfields. The author was describing the green swaying stalks of the corn as the breeding place for enormous blackbirds that demons rode into a nearby farm town. I almost choked on the words before putting the book upside down and the binding inward. This was not what I planned. I turned my hat backward and hoped for some help from somewhere.

At the end of the rows were walls. I bent down with my hands on my knees, breathing in and out like a bellows. Saliva pooled in the space between my lower lip and my teeth. As I wheezed I remembered I went to the library for kayaks, for the right way to leave this place. So I went downstairs looking for the travel and adventure section.

Downstairs, I found the travel sign above a stack along the wall, and next to a book about the migration pattern of cranes I found a book about canoeing and the rivers around Lincoln. It seemed right so I pulled it down, leaning against the stack, reading it. I figured kayaks and canoes were similar. But the book did not work, or maybe it was me, and I couldn't get the words to stick. Trying again and again, I read and reread the same passage, mouthing the words. But it didn't matter. The words held no meaning.

The pictures of rivers, trees and water helped though. They conveyed meaning and seemed attractive enough to be reason for leaving, so I put the book in my backpack and zipped it up.

As I walked out of the building the alarm went off from the book but I thought it was just the ringing in my ears and the buzzing in my head getting louder. When the doors shut the sound faded and, I don't know, maybe the librarians thought they would stay away from a wreck like me, but they didn't come out. It was probably good, I couldn't tell the difference between their alarm and the sound of my head crying out for Carmen to take off the clamps.

So I walked on and out in the sun. The burning grew stronger, my eyes unable to take the light. I pulled my hat around and down against my eyebrows, walking away from the library, falling farther away but still moving fast, my head tilted down and my eyes watching the rolling sidewalk in front of me. I wanted to disappear down a hole and bring the city with me; I would have walked into an open manhole without caring. I wanted an earthquake to open up or a wave to wash it all clean. Anything to change the way I felt.

Whenever I looked up swirls of images tortured me and I winced and let out silent screams. The pain turned me delusional to the point of hallucination. Heat waves rose off the sidewalks as purple and orange flames, the sidewalks asked me to lie upon them, my face on the concrete, sweating fluid to the drains and out to the river. Under the surface, gravity, a giant with rippled muscles, pulled the strings and chains attached to my body, laughing at my struggle. Around me the sky loomed down blue and bright, heavy and savage, the clouds pillows over my face.

I fought against it all until I stopped outside of a bus stop, sweating, breathing hard, holding the straps of my backpack white-knuckle tight and swaying. Dazed, with my mouth open,

I looked up.

No help from up there. No help from anywhere. I was going to have to do it on my own. Turning to the right, looking away from the library, a man in a gray suit and sunglasses, briefcase in hand, came bearing down on me. I couldn't see his eyes but I knew they were black and focused straight on me. This made me panic, turn the corner, and flatten my back to the wall.

The businessman walked across the street with one hand on his briefcase and one hand on his cell phone. With my back flat to the building, after he passed, I put my hands on my knees and bent over.

13

Down the street, a building from the college—one of the glorious rectangles that was set on its end—stood tall in my view. It caused me to remember my class schedule and then to remember that it was Monday morning. After straightening myself out, I took the paper from my pocket, unfolded then read from it. It said if I hurried I could still make it to English. I was always good at English. The problem, though, was that I still didn't know where my classes were. Maybe, I thought, I could still give it a try. I walked toward campus to find my classroom.

As I walked down the sidewalk I held the straps of my backpack tight in my fists. I pulled them down, my knuckles white, just as gravity pulled the strings to work against my walking. But suddenly I experienced a strong aversion toward my destination. The thought of people, of being social, and the unavoidable talking associated with them created a wind of resistance that staggered me as it gusted. With the wind pushing into me, I leaned against it, fighting the force, and add that to what gravity would have me do, lie down or find a hole to dive into, and my strength faded—the elements of resistance stronger.

After a block or two of fighting I gave up the idea of going to class. The forces telling me to stop were fierce, plus I knew plenty of excuses. It was syllabus week. Something I had only heard about, but I knew two things about college, that you went to class if you wanted to, and that the first week was syllabus week. I repeated it to myself. Syllabus week. It sounded right. It sounded like a good excuse.

Alcohol could help my headache. I decided instead of going to class I would head over to the gas station and see if I could get somebody to buy me some vodka or whiskey. Yet still the hallucinations remained. I watched as the sun scorched holes in my skin that smoldered and smoked like rising volcanoes.

As holes opened in the ground all around me it seemed important to tell someone about what I was seeing. To find a girl to talk to and share with her what I was feeling—a girl to hold my head up, to get excited about. A girl to take my mind off this feeling, maybe even bring me to her version of reality. At that point it was surrendered that my reality was unrecoverable—I needed someone else's eyes.

After walking for what seemed like miles to the gas station, I stopped when I came to it. I didn't want to go in right away—I more just wanted to find someone who could buy me a bottle of anything for an extra dollar. It seemed awful I was looking for that, but if I wanted a drink I didn't really have any other choice. Around the outside of the gas station a woman in a suit pumped gas into a four-door sedan and an old man wiped the windows on his motor home.

There wasn't anyone in sight with the proper qualifications to buy so I went inside. Harsh lighting and the smell of processed meat instantly sickened me. A young guy, a construction worker type with a red ponytail, worked behind the counter. I walked to the refrigerator door, opened it, then turned and watched the cashier. He rang up a pack of cigarettes for a girl and I wondered if he would sell to me. I imagined he would've been sympathetic, he seemed to be the partying type. I mean he sported a ponytail and worked at a gas station. I was sure he drank himself to sleep. He looked up at me. I stood in front of the open refrigerator door then closed it, went over to the magazine rack, stared at the vacant eyes of the celebrities, then looked up at him. He was filling out some form on the counter. I looked over the store. It was empty. I went over to the liquor bottles and found the biggest plastic bottle of vodka I could. I didn't want to hesitate, so to make it confident I picked it up quickly and headed straight for the counter. I set it down. He looked at me and I looked at him. He smirked, then told me how much it was. I unfolded a wadded up ten dollar bill, handed it to him and walked out with the bottle and put it in my backpack as I left the store.

Walking down the street, away from the gas station, I looked for someplace to go, someplace like a park or an alley or a hole to crawl into. It didn't matter where, I just wanted to feel like I knew where I was going, like I had a destination. I would have gone anywhere—into a tree house, an abandoned warehouse, a trapdoor—it didn't matter, just anywhere to drink the vodka and maybe make a friend.

Down the city streets and under the green leaves of late August I walked for a while longer—still in the downtown part of the city—until I came to a school playground. The hope of alcohol distracted me from the pain in my head; I could see the end of the pain coming soon. The playground offered the standard equipment: swings, teeter-totter, merry-go-round, all of them old and rusted. Green weeds grew around the poles that held the equipment in the ground, but what interested me the most was the slide. Up on top—it was one of those curly whirlygiggers, striped yellow and red—was a shelter with a roof. The stairs I climbed up went right through the center of the curling slide.

Under the roof I opened the bottle, turning the lid until I tore it from the plastic ring. I took a drink. It burned my mouth and nose, down my throat, almost choking me. I gagged on the second drink, but I focused my attention on the bottle and the drinking, and it made me forget quite a bit of what was on my mind. It was hot with the liquor in my feverish body. My body was tired when I was climbing the stairs of the slide but after the vodka I felt no fatigue and my mind recharged.

Under the roof I looked around the walls at the words written inside the slide. I could see hearts, initials, Fuck This Town, John

Was Here. I opened my throat and dumped some more in. It burned so bad. My eyes watered and I wiped the corners.

It didn't take long for the alcohol to get on top of me. I watched as the shadows shifted, turned, and grew longer while I sat there, not moving, just drinking and suffocating. It was not until I drank it all—finished the bottle, gagging the hardest on the last few drops—before I slid down the metal plates of the slide.

At first my sweaty clothes stuck to the metal, but I scooted until I loosened from it then slid down. I hit the ground with my feet but my knees weren't ready so I fell into the gravel. Stunned a little, I sat there in the gravel wanting the ride to last longer—for me to fall farther.

The falling felt good and I thought about going down again, only I didn't want to return to the suffocation of the inside of the top of the slide. Instead, my legs wobbly, I walked out of the park, across the gravel and lawn and to the sidewalk, heading toward the university. The sun grew stronger, pressing against my shoulders and the back of my head.

I stopped in the doorway of an apartment building for the shade and sat down. I thought about how I used to have so much energy, how I used to be articulate. I thought about the courage I did or didn't have, and my friends, and I thought about this time that I kept returning to, a memory my mind loved to recreate.

It happened the weekend before I left, a night with my friends, when I still knew them, where we all got together to throw a bonfire party in the shed at Jake's cabin. The night started off normal. We started drinking about the same time we always did. Building the fire, throwing things that explode into it, then, and this is the part I think that left the lasting impression, I went outside to call Sierra and when I came back inside I saw Lena standing across from the fire. We never touched before but I always thought she was cute. In one of the cheesiest moves of my life I crossed around the side of the fire and walked at her as she smiled and so did I, and I walked into her and put my hand on her neck and kissed her, before either of us could say anything. I can be real chivalrous sometimes. Even though that moment was brief, I felt more sure of that action than any in my life.

After hearing some movement behind me in the apartment building I came out of the fire memory and walked on, head down, into the sun. Lena with the heart-shaped face, Lena one of my favorite memories.

At that moment, as I walked down the sidewalk I wanted to find a girl to hang out with more than anything. The university was getting closer and thinking about her made me feel exposed, raw, like skin peeled away from bone and it seemed everyone was staring at a walking skeleton shedding its skin.

As I walked I saw her face in the sidewalk, and when I looked up the rectangles of the university were larger in the distance. The alcohol still held on, causing my eyes to move slowly back and forth across the approaching landscape. They fixated upon the dorms, the rising stone structures penetrating the skyline, and I headed toward the one I heard was supposed to be for the fun kids. The coed dorm where all the parties raged.

A guy and a girl sat smoking on the steps as I went in the doors of the dorms, past the check-in counter and into the empty elevator. I hit a number, leaning against the wall as it rose, and it stopped somewhere in the middle. I got out and went down the hall to the bathroom. With the stall door closed I sat down on the toilet to plan my next move.

After thinking about her I decided I'd walk up and down the halls until I found something going on. In the hallway, smells of incense, popcorn, and the sounds of laughter and bottles clinking against other bottles blurred past, entering and leaving my body as I walked through. All the doors were closed. I walked from end to end of each hall, at the end of the hall taking the stairs up to the next floor. I did this until I came to the top of the building, then went through a door and took the steps up to the roof.

Out on the roof I walked out to the edge and looked down. I imagined what it would be like to land on the street and thought about the sound of my body landing on the sidewalk.

I've always liked the idea of falling. As I grew up I loved jumping out of swings, pulling on the chains to launch from the seat of the swing. I never minded the ankle sting—just falling through the air was worth it, as close as you could get to flying.

That day, standing there on the ledge, I thought about jumping. I wondered if I would scream, if my mouth would be open. On the ledge, the wind gusting, making it that much more intense, I knew I was drunk, that I didn't trust my balance and I thought I should sit down. So I slung my legs over the edge of the stone ledge. I held my knees with my hands as I stared through the gaps between my shoes. I was thinking about fighting the vertigo, thinking about the feeling in my stomach and that if a girl pushed me it was over, thinking about keeping the courage to stay on the ledge. When I looked up I saw a crowd on the sidewalk forming, looking up at me. I stood up quick, too quick, became lightheaded and a gust of wind came up and I stumbled.

I stumbled away from the ledge and fell onto the tar-covered roof on my side. I turned onto my back and looked up to the sky, where the blue seemed to purple and darken. But it was just me passing out. So to fight it I crawled onto my knees then stood and walked to the door I had gone through to get on the roof.

When I opened the door to go down the stairs the resident assistant was coming up at me, taking the stairs three at a time. He stopped when we met.

I made to walk past him but he moved to block my way. He put his hand on my chest. I looked him in the eyes.

"You need to wait here until security comes. Someone called the police," the assistant said.

We waited in silence until the security guard opened the door to the stairwell, radioed on his walkie-talkie something about locating the perpetrator, then approached me.

He took me down the hall, down the elevator to the first floor, then to the main office of the dormitory where I met the person in charge of the building—an older lady with glasses who sat behind a wooden desk covered in papers. Her credentials and pictures of her family riding horses hung on the walls.

She stared at her desk, not looking at me when I came in. With the tension in the room I could tell the first thing she wanted to do was yell. I took a seat in front of her desk and slouched.

She took off her glasses then put them back on, snapping her head up then—

"You're in serious trouble. That crowd thought you wanted to give us a show."

"I didn't even see...I didn't even see any cameras. I mean if they thought I was going to jump off there would have been something, right? The paparazzi?"

She paused then, looking down at her desk. She picked up a pen and wrote for a minute. The silence was disgusting. "I'm going to recommend you undergo a psychological evaluation if you wish to stay on as a student here at Lincoln. That is standard procedure for a situation like this. But first you will be required to." Sirens from a fire truck or an ambulance outside split her sentence. "Those are here for you." This made me feel small, which I deserved. She adjusted her glasses and looked down at her desk. The tension in the room thickened, gravity fighting a hard battle against atmosphere and temperature. "I'm going to recommend you meet with the Dean. He'll expel you, or make you take this year off, reapply. If you're lucky. Though, if you agree to see a counselor we might be able to keep you on. That all depends on you. You will meet Dean Chambers Wednesday morning at 9:00. If you have class you can have him sign a note for your professor. That is if you are still a student here. And do not be late or miss it, or I will expel you myself. Do you have anything else you want to say?"

I could tell she wanted me to apologize or something.

"I needed to sit down. It was windy."

I walked out of the office feeling awesome. The drunk turned stale. I think I burned it up by sweating all the alcohol out during that meeting. It sucked, either I met with the dean in the morning or I was kicked out of the university. Sweet. I needed that.

Not only did my head start to hurt but the rest of my body wanted the sleep I'd been depriving it of for days. I walked down the hall away from her office and through the dorm lobby. Part of the crowd from outside stood in front of the elevators watching me. I hate it when people stare.

A reporter from the school newspaper asked me my name and if he could ask me a question. I walked past without speaking. He said he would look me up in the student directory and give me a call. Good luck, I said.

14

I went out of the dorms with no direction, walking off aimless until I remembered the kayak. It came to me in a yellow flash of color. I could see it spraying water as the nose slapped against the rapids I dropped it down and could almost feel the cool water coating my face.

My feet should have ached from walking. But my body detached from my brain, almost as if they were not in communication anymore. My feet felt far away and numb. They could have been prosthetics with how dull and detached they felt as I pounded them down the sidewalk for miles toward the kayak.

The air in the sporting goods store smelled thick and old, slightly less decrepit than an antique store. All it needed was a quarter inch of dust and you could believe no one had gone in there for a decade. The aisles stayed stocked easily, the racks full of coats, the shelves piled with sweaters. Maybe they didn't move too much merchandise in and out; I don't remember seeing anyone other than the old man shuffling around behind the counter.

He never spoke much when I was in there, just the standard, inevitable "How are you?" and my standard, ineffective "good."

When I gave the old man my card for the rest of the money, he bent his head down and looked over his glasses at me. I looked up and met his eyes then checked the pattern on the tile. All I wanted to do was get my kayak, find a river, and float out to the ocean. After the look he ran my card, made me sign the slip, then sold it to me and we went to the back to get it down from the wall. I could feel myself getting excited. The body was bright yellow with a black hole in the center where I would sit.

Before the old man took his side down off the hook he stopped. He sort of breathed in and out, looking at me, then he went on with pulling it down.

We took the kayak off the wall, brought it to the front, and set it down in front of the door.

"What's the best way to carry it?"

"Over your head. Just like a canoe."

I picked it up, holding it over my hat with my hands and he held the door, looking at my shoes as I walked out. The thing was heavy and my balance was off, kind of clumsy, but I found if I walked fast I could keep it steady enough. After the first few steps I could hear the old man lock the doors behind me and the slap of the open sign being switched to closed.

Carrying the kayak to the hotel made me tired after about a block so I sat it down in the middle of the sidewalk and sat on it. The gray dusk got on top of me as it deepened. Dusk does that—if the day went well then I'm okay, content with the approaching night, but if it went bad then it's almost as if the night is coming too fast.

But it's also a second chance, and I watched the shadows grow for only a few minutes before I got up and picked up the kayak. I wanted to get to the hotel before it got dark. It came on quick as I walked down the sidewalk.

Once I came to the hotel, I took the kayak up in the elevator and into the room with no small effort. It stood up in the corner of the room, standing guard as I climbed up on the center of the mattress and stared into the television screen, my knees locked and my hands in my back pockets. I don't know what I watched but I know when I looked up the night had thickened and I needed a drink or a girl to run across a bridge with. Staying in the hotel room all night was not going to happen, there was no way. I got down from the bed then headed out of the hotel.

Down the street a few blocks people waited in line to get

into a bar. Walking to it made me dream of the girl inside, the one that would save my life, dance with me until she wanted me to be next to her for the rest of her existence. Fate wanted me to sneak into the bar and find her, the most amazing person that would take me into her life and we would always smile when we told our friends about how we met when she saved me from getting thrown out for looking too young.

When I approached the bouncer he asked for my identification. I told him I lost it and he said I would have to find it if I wanted to get in. His arms were bigger than my thighs. A stone wall, he ignored my feeble attempt at persuasion. So I said fine and turned around. When I looked out to the street there was a couple—a blonde girl in a white skirt with her boyfriend wearing a black t-shirt—flowing out of a yellow taxicab. They were what I wanted more than anything. I hailed the cab. The smell of the blonde remained; her perfume murdered me. I told the driver to take me to my car.

The taxi driver slammed back the plastic and took off. The smell of the woman faded away. I figured the driver knew what I meant with how fast he was driving—he took a corner hard enough to slide me into the door.

When I righted myself I tapped on the window. Nothing happened. I knocked again. He slid back the plastic and I could see his bloodshot eyes staring into mine.

"What's your name?"

He stared into my eyes for a second before he slid the glass shut. It took the wind out of me and I tapped but he didn't open it. I tried but again he left it closed. The driver wanted no talking, no interaction. He must have been tired, or maybe he just didn't like the looks of me.

We came to a stop at one of the lots—he just stopped in the middle wherever he felt like it. The lot didn't look right but he stopped and got out. The cab felt suffocating and empty in that brief moment when he came to the door.

The taxi driver watched my hands the whole time and even when I took the money from my wallet and handed it to him he never looked in my eyes. He said nothing then returned to his cab.

After he drove off I watched the red lights shrink into dots then disappear. Walking up and down the rows reading license plates and bumper stickers I finally figured out my car was at the frat. That was a waste of energy. But at that point my energy was something spareable, something I could afford to waste.

Streetlights hummed over the sidewalks, and the idea of walking over to the frat worried me. The fraternity brothers were looking for me, wondering what happened, and if anyone saw me I would have to answer their questions. The thought of it was frightening.

Most of the lights were on in the old frat house hotel. Voices came through some of the open windows on the second and third stories. I went around the back and somehow without seeing anyone I made it to the parking lot.

When I came up to my car there was a note under the windshield wiper. It was written on a wet piece of white paper and looked as if it had been stuck there for a few days.

Carrick, where the hell you been partner? Bangin' some beaver?

McPherson

That was all it said. I crumpled the paper and let it fall next to my tire before I got in and the hell away from there as fast as my car would take me. I always want to get as far away from something as I can when I leave somewhere, but that note made it even easier. I had the thought, if you're going to get away, then it should be really far away, so I drove out, way out of Lincoln, until I was on dirt roads and under white-yellow stars. The rocks on the dirt roads kicked up into the undercarriage of my car every once in a while, making a loud popping sound.

The night laughed at my headlights—meager attempts at illumination on the dirt roads splitting the fields—and in my rearview mirror a cloud of dust arose that blocked my view of the city. Around me the landscape was the same countryside I had driven past my entire life; Scottsbluff was four hundred miles from Lincoln but it didn't matter, the same crops grew on both ends—corn, alfalfa and beans. The only difference now was that they had rain on this end and their crops could actually grow.

As I drove farther away from the city I had the feeling that I might not know the way back if I went too far out. Waking up a farmer and asking him the best way to the city would be humiliating, but interesting, so I drove a little longer until Lincoln disappeared.

Then I found a good place to pull over off the side of the road. A few feet up from where I stopped, a canal ran off to the left. A dirt road lined the canal—the farmers could check on their irrigation with their pickups during the season with it. The irrigation season would be ending in a week or two, the crops all grown out and starting to turn and ripen for the harvest.

I accelerated then turned left onto the road. It was narrow and smooth with two ruts from the repeated use of the farmers' pickups. The thought I came up with was to drive down the road until I was alone enough to have some time to figure out why I could not stop sweating, or how to get rid of the burning halo that constricted around my temples. It seemed that I should be able to control it, to make it stop, that it was a controllable thing, but really every hour was another turn of the crank. I thought once I was in familiar terrain—I mean every cornfield really is the same—I would be comfortable enough to figure out to control it, and then I could figure out how to sleep. I thought I might walk down a row of corn until I got in the middle of the field then fall on my back and stare up at the stars through the leaves until the claustrophobia and humidity forced me to sleep. My cell phone went past the point of beeping when I stopped my car next to a check in the canal with a sectional dam to raise the water level. The headlights died and the silence of the night swept down to fill my car then strangle me. I got out before it could and the sound of the water flowing through the check came up from the bank.

I walked out across the concrete bridge spanning the canal to the middle and looked into the oncoming water. It moved slowly like how a snake moves. The light of the moon reflected off the calm water and angled away from where I stood. Moonlight on the snake's back.

Turning around, the white water churned in the rumbling wake of the waterfall that the check caused. It frothed and swirled. Looking at it made me want to jump into the calm end and tumble through the waterfall. Feel the water fill my ears and pull me through the check, drive me down to the bottom, spin my body. Listening to the water roar from there was the only sound that could be louder than the ringing in my ears. But the ringing held a different pitch, a higher tone, and the two sounds did not blend in harmony.

Standing there in the center of the bridge I watched the water until I felt more alone, more desperate than ever before. The feeling attacked in waves, repeating cannonballs fired into my throat. At that moment I wanted to call any girl I knew so I took out my phone to go through the numbers. But I could not get it to turn on and I got anxious, my heart freezing, and I hit the button but it would not turn on so, over it, I turned and threw it across the water. Chucked it into the calm end. It skipped like a rock three times, leaving circles, then disappeared under the surface, passing through the falls, sinking to the bottom.

As I stood looking into the moonlight reflect off the smoothing ripples, at the water becoming calmer, I thought about my parents and how I should have called them when I got to Lincoln. They for sure wanted to know how college was, what I was doing. But I'd have to go to town if I wanted to call them and I wasn't ready for that. Being out in the country helped a little and staying sounded better.

At my feet, the concrete of the bridge contained a little moisture on it and it looked cool, like it could help. The water flowed with the same roar underneath as I lay down on it, looking up, trying to guess at the blinking constellations. All the stars blurred and swirled together—putting them into a constellation required an organization my mind could not make.

I lay there for a minute, thinking how much better it would be to be on the canal with my kayak. Yellow and gleaming in the sunlight under the green leaves of the trees rolling by overhead—no sound. A smile grew in the corners of my eyes.

Something about that kayak, about the pull of the river, picked me up off the bridge, the thought growing strong in my mind until I was in my car then driving back to Lincoln. Focus remained on the yellow piece of fiberglass standing up in the corner of the hotel room, blocking out all light and thought, tunneling toward the kayak.

When I got to my room I went in then took the kayak from the corner, drug it out, fighting it a little and set it in the hall. As it made noise from setting it on the floor the faces of my parents appeared on the ground in front of me. They knew questions that needed to be answered.

Inside the hotel room, gathering the courage to dial the numbers required counting to three four separate times before making the call.

A woman cleared her throat.

"Carrick," she said, "call tomorrow, and go to sleep."

If the conversation would have lasted any longer the truth would have come through, but ending it then saved it from my tone of voice becoming earnest and revealing. Hanging up, then staring at the phone, my thoughts remained on her, who rolled over after she hung up, said "Carrick" to him, who snorted then went back to sleep. She kept her eyes open until the stare broke.

Shaking it off, I ran to the hall and took the kayak down the elevator and out of the hotel to my car. I carried it overhead out to the parking lot then found my car and set it down next to it.

With open doors I tried to put it in by laying the front seat down and pulling the headrest off, but I still couldn't get it to fit. Through the trunk with the backseats down failed as well. Straps were the only answer so, giving up, I took it back up to my room.

As it's weight shifted awkwardly from front to back carrying it to the elevator, the thought that made me feel ridiculous hit me: I didn't have the oars for it anyway.

You cannot steer a kayak without oars.

Feeling foolish from that, and from the lack of sleep crashing my memory, I don't know what I did from when I put the kayak in my room until the next morning. The memory escapes, flies away into the abyss. I guess I paced the room with the television on. That was the behavior that would most likely result from my head's condition—which was on fire with an anaconda wrapped around it. Laying down and closing my eyes would only produce panging flashes of yellow and orange light that burned the inside of my forehead as if they were microwave waves or the end of a branding iron. There was no way to sleep with that going on.

15

When the pink of dawn hinted on the east side of Lincoln, I went out to the early morning dew and the sound of birds. It would have been beautiful under better conditions, the city still waking up, only a few cars on the street, a wet coat of dew on the parking meters.

But the sun hurt too much to look up for longer than a couple of seconds as I walked around downtown with my hat pulled down tight and the book from the library in my backpack, looking for anywhere to go, anything to do. The mornings were more endurable than the afternoons, but the naked sunlight still caused thoughts of digging holes or jumping into wells.

I walked around most of downtown Lincoln and I liked the scene: business men and women wearing suits, carrying briefcases off to important jobs; the city buses bringing people to work in fumes of exhaust; a steady increasing flow of traffic and noise. The air felt pure and clean and new. I liked all of it and it made me feel good to walk the sidewalks past the smiling people who said hi to me despite my pale and bloodshot face. Starting their days caffeinated and energized, ready to work, they must have been happy to not look as beat as me. Criss-crossed, wooden oars popped up into my head and made me feel just as dumb as last night but now there was action to take.

Turning around and walking back the way I came, when I made it over to the store the lights were on, but the doors were locked and the closed sign remained. A sale sign offered summer clothing at forty percent off. I went around back to see if I could knock and have the owner, my old friend, open up.

Pounding on the back door took most of my energy, and after I knocked I sat down in the alley and took out the book in my backpack. Resting and reading seemed to equate. As I read, for the first time in three days I felt tired. Shoulders resting against the brick wall, sliding down farther and farther until the backpack became a pillow. I read on but the words blurred and I put the book down. Black clouds swirled, gathering like birds. I turned my head to the side and closed my eyes.

Orange and yellow waves shot out, piercing the first few seconds, but their intensity faded and they became pale and warm. Sleep would have won out if not for the shadow and smell that came over me.

"What readin'?"

The voice sounded so nightmarish, so shrill and craggy, it took a moment for me to decide whether it was real or a dream.

"Does it look like I'm," I stopped when I opened my eyes and in the same instant smelled her. The size of her with all her bags, clothes and crazed grayish-brown hair would have been less imposing but she stood on top of me. She smelled putrid and raw, like an ashtray made from rotting fish. It attacked me when I took a breath but by far the most abrasive aspect of her was her voice.

She spat a little when she spoke and some landed on me. The first time that happened made me sit up quick. She bent down to get the book between my feet, picked it up, looked at the back flap of the book jacket, then dropped it. Her insistence on knowing what book was in my hands seemed strange.

Watching me put the book in my bag, stand up, turn a shoulder to her, and make to walk away, she called after me. Turning back and jamming my hands into my front pockets, my eyes swept over her. She wore red sweatpants with silver tape around the cuffs and carried plastic grocery bags under her arm like a purse. It was sad, she held herself in the way a woman does, and she *was* still a woman, but she had become much more abused and worn-out than most.

When I made to check my pockets and shake my head at the same time my mind spawned the gross thought that she needed money and she was also old enough to buy alcohol. The ugly idea came to me to get her to go along with my plan. I stood up and took out a five dollar bill from my wallet. She huffed and grunted, sputtering a little. I held the green bill up to her with my hands, then ripped it in half. She groaned and pulled on her hair.

"Okay," I said. "I'm going to give you the rest of this, but you have to do something for me."

I held out half to her as her eyes bounced from one hand to the other. She took the half and balled it into her fist then held out her other hand for the second half. She huffed and grunted, moving toward me until the torn bill went into my pocket. If I had looked at my Grandfather's painting then the top block would have been greenish brown and the bottom the color of piss.

"You know what whiskey is?"

She nodded fast, up and down like a little kid. Kathy got all weird then. Like super weird. She puffed out her chest and, in a warbled, throaty, mucous-filled voice, sang. One hand holding half of the five dollar bill, the other lifted in an emphatic expression of the opera moment, she belted out what sounded like Italian. Like something you need the little binoculars on a stick to see.

Kathy stumbled at first, choking on herself until she cleared a path for, and the more I think about it, the more I think it really was a beautiful opera voice. Seriously, where the voice came from and how she could go from talking like a witch to singing like an angel is anyone's guess, but god could she sing. I hate the opera and I don't use the word beautiful much—but dammit her voice was so good. Almost as if her fate was compensated with a gift that no matter what happened to her she would always have.

I was stunned—she was good but loud and behind the shop I wanted to come back to, plus we made a deal, so I took her by the arm. She resisted at first, but I led her away from the store as she sirened full opera soprano loud next to me. Her spit, though, was a byproduct of her singing that remained crucial to avoid.

We walked a little way like that, me escorting her, and Kathy kept it going for most of the alleyway but then her voice dried up and she coughed as we turned onto the street. My hand fell from her arm as she bent a little to clear her throat.

Then she sort of regained her old self and froze in the middle of the sidewalk, looking straight ahead, not moving. A blank look, almost as if her brain stopped firing, swept across her face. I pulled on her arm but she didn't move. She stared straight into the ground, boring a hole to the center of the earth.

Her head snapped up as she asked the air in front of her—

"Where goin'?"

I held up my half of the five-dollar bill to her face and her mouth opened but there was no look of recognition on her face, just spittle in the corners of her mouth. The bill hung in front of her eyes. She stared until she opened her fist and looked at the other half in her hand.

As if the signal in her brain was rerouted, Kathy turned and took off shuffling in her broken flip-flops toward the main avenue of the business district. She had not made any indication that she knew where she was going and at first I thought she was leading me in the wrong direction. But she walked with my half of the five dollar bill so it made sense to stick with her.

Together, with me following right behind her and trying not to step on her sandals, we walked toward the high-rise office buildings. They were a lot smaller in Lincoln than in other cities, but they were still there, with their stacked mirrored windows and acronym corporate logos.

We approached a convenience store with a neon beer sign in the window, the slogan written over a waterfall. It surprised me, Kathy knew where she was going—she would have walked right in but I sped up and turned in front of her. She looked at me as if she had never seen me before until I held up the money. I spoke in a low voice, holding the money in front of her.

I took out ten dollars from my wallet.

"Whiskey," I said, "as much as you can get."

She took the money and went inside.

Sitting on the sidewalk outside of the store, waiting for what seemed like a long time as the sun shot up hot and the dew retreated, I should have gotten nervous, the feeling wanted to build in me, but there was not any connection with my brain and my body anymore.

After noticing how numb I had become, I watched Kathy come out. Her plastic bags hit the door as she left, slowing her a bit, but she hurried on, walking faster than before, her shuffle replaced with a short, quick step. She went the other way, away from me. She worried me enough to hop up and walk quick to catch her.

I followed her down the street and around the corner to the alley where I caught up to her by taking her arm. She wheezed and grunted and she took her arm from me, not even glancing at me as she shuffled away fast. The five-dollar bill was the only chance to stop her.

"Kathy," I said, dancing to move in front and hold up the halved bill to her.

"Kathy," I said, stopping in front of her and planting my legs wide.

She pivoted like a robot and tried to walk around me, but back-pedaling kept the dollar bill in front of her.

I moved the bill closer to her face.

It didn't matter, she wouldn't stop. My legs ached from walking backwards so I slowed to let her pass. In her plastic bag I could see two bottles of something. I reached into the bag and took out the bottle, the bottle I thought was mine. It was pink plastic capped on a silver canister. A bottle of aerosol hairspray. She grabbed for it.

“Kathy,” I said, holding the hairspray, “I said whiskey.”

“Not Kat’y,” she said.

No response for this, I let her take the bottle of hairspray then shuffle on. Watching her slide down the street with the two pink plastic caps sticking out of the bag she carried like a purse, I crumpled the half of the five dollars and let it fall to the ground. Neither of us got the money yet Kathy would have firm hair.

Turning around, I walked down the street the way I came and as the day wore on the streets seemed quiet, less alive. There were more cars but all the people that had been on the streets were up in their offices working.

Work would have been good for me then if my body was able to do it, which was doubtful. There was not much of a chance I could focus long enough to complete a task—the thoughts concerning me the most, filling up my head, were of leaving or getting rid of the pain in my temples.

If there would be no drinking, no whiskey, then the oars for kayaking could be obtained. By that time, after that diversion with Kathy, the store would be open. It didn’t take me long to get to the alley. The library book I left behind was still there when I walked up to the back of the store and it went into my backpack. Thinking about where the closest river was—north, it seemed, was the way—I went around the block to the front of the store.

A bell sounded as the door opened and I walked in. The old man looked up at me, turning his eyes up to look over his glasses, a slight smile moving one corner of his mouth. Before words came from mine, he moved over to the oars. Exposure of my naivety stung and I pulled down my hat, not making eye contact.

After throwing out a knowing look, the old man took two paddles down from the wall and the store started to feel bright and hot. It was as if the lights were replaced with spotlights and the particles of light they emitted were microwave rays. Sweat filled my pores and leaked from the holes in my skin, running out into the hair on my body as the blackbirds flew in to cloud my eyes. Balance dripped out onto the tile. When the man handed me an oar I took it and used it as a crutch to hold myself up—the sweat from my palm coating the plastic end I leaned upon.

The old man looked at me, cleared his throat, and I knew he wanted to ask if I was okay, but I started asking him questions. More than anything, my objective was to keep him from getting worried about me and start asking me where my parents were or my age or anything, really. Sweat ran into my shirt collar and filled up the band in my hat. Seriously, it felt bright as hell in there, as if the door was shut, the timer set on defrost, the start button pressed, the light on, and my body spun on a plastic plate in the center.

Running out of conversation about plastic versus wood, we split and took the oars up to the counter. My oar served well as a walking stick though it was short and it made me hunch like an old lady.

After hanging onto the counter while I paid for the oars, I asked the man if he could provide a strap or rack for my car and he went over to the wall while I waited, leaning against the counter.

Resting as he brought the box over and rang it up, I watched him put it and one of the oars in a bag, leaving an oar out for me to walk. I guess he knew. I put it all on my card, scribbled my name on a white paper receipt and stumbled out. The oars and the box together were awkward but with one hand on the oar and the other carrying the bag I made it to the hotel.

In late August the corn turns yellow as it ripens for the harvest. But the trees are green until October, so when you drive out into the country the trees are dots of green on the yellow background of the cornfields. Green on gold. As the strapped yellow kayak cut down the gray highway, out to the left, the sun changed from gold to orange with pink tendrils on a darkening blue.

The main river in the state ran west to east from Scottsbluff to Lincoln. It started where the snow melted in the mountains west of Scottsbluff and flowed across the state to the big water that carried it all down to the ocean. The river the kayak pointed towards ran along the north side of the state—so I thought if I headed that direction I'd find it soon enough. The sun would die in a little over an hour and the idea of floating under the stars seemed good.

My car passed row after row and field after field of corn. Not a lot of cars on the two-lane highway out of Lincoln, but that wasn't surprising. Here everyone has a lot of space to breathe. Driving down the road, if there was anyone on the highway, they would raise one finger to wave—the farmer's salute.

The first thing I came upon on my side of the road was an old, beat-up pickup truck. The old thing moved slowly down the road, probably about thirty-five miles an hour. Before getting close it was easy to know the driver was a farmer—I could tell from the wooden shovel handle sticking out of the corner of the pickup box.

Pulling around to the left, I passed him slow, and I could see the man driving the truck was in his 50s. A hard-working man. He turned his weathered, mustached face at me and waved with one finger up on the steering wheel. The wave of the man who waves at every car he passes.

To me it made sense why he drove so slowly—he was in-between fields, done checking on one sprinkler or ditch and moving on to the other, where he would park at the top of the field, get the shovel off the back of the truck, walk down the bank in that stiff, overworked way. The work of a farmer during season can be as exhausting as any. I could imagine a cigarette hanging out of his mouth or a chew in his lip as he moved down the bank, looking out across the field, surveying his work. He would shoulder the shovel and walk down the ditch, checking that the water moved down the field right, making sure the crops got the water they needed, that rows were not broke over, that no weeds stopped the water. He would have to do some digging—pulling up his jeans as he bent down to dig in efficient, violent jabs at the dirt, though his back had hurt for thirty years from the constant labor. He would get himself up after the digging and move on down the ditch, checking the rows, fixing the cuts, making sure the corn got its water.

As he faded in my mirror my thoughts returned to the river and the fiberglass overhead. The straps held down the kayak better than I thought they would—they didn't move much, the only thing I noticed was the sound they made as they hummed in the wind. It was hot and I could see the heat lines rise on the highway, shimmering the horizon. The water in the river would cool my burning head.

All the skin on my face seemed heavy and full of hot water, holding it out the window helped, but the wind watered my eyes and my driving suffered for it so I held it out only for brief flashes. The sky on the horizon became the color of the feeling in my head.

Sunsets hold more beauty than possible for me to absorb, so instead the dashed yellow lines in the center of the highway held the weight of my sight for the length of the drive, until up ahead a long patch of trees down in a valley stretched across the horizon. The sight of the river flooded my imagination with possible outcomes. The kayak could take me to the stern of a riverboat, to the back porch of a southern plantation, to the fan boats and alligators of backcountry swamps. It could take me as far as the oars could row and the fiberglass could float.

Ahead cottonwoods spread out in both directions, the green clumps of leaves with white balls of wispy cotton resting atop thick trunks. They blocked the sunset as I drove into the cover of them and onto a bridge. Centered above the river, I slowed down to look at the water, and after seeing it flow I drove across and turned left onto a dirt path that took me to the water's edge. It was shady under the cottonwoods and I could hear frogs talking.

I drove down the bank to the end of the path then parked and got out. As soon as I stepped out of my car the frogs quieted. I could hear the water and it was cool under the shade of the trees. The bank was gradual, covered with short grass with dried bits that stuck in my socks. The cottonwoods dropped white cottonflakes that landed on my windshield and caught in my hair.

Around my car, where I parked, the grass had grown tall and I stepped it down to get over to the straps on the roof. The cotton came down in flurries when the wind blew. I unstrapped the kayak from my car, carried it down to the water and set it down, then I went to my car for the oars. My head still hurt, all the activity increasing the weight and pressure.

When I took the oars from the car down to the kayak, a weird thing happened. I stood at the end trying to convince myself to shove it in, but my motivation disappeared—I didn't want to put the kayak in the water. The cotton fell around me, landing in my hair; a grasshopper jumped into the water and swam with its legs kicking. I looked to the swaying branches of the trees.

Instead, lowering myself into the hole in the middle and strapping in, I sat on the bank of the river, on the water, in the dark. My legs fit into the hollow of the fiberglass okay and staring at the opposite bank, sitting there, with the water going by, for the first time in days I fell asleep. Crashed out hard into featureless dreams.

16

When I awoke the stars were out—they rippled in waves as though blobs of paint on a billowing curtain. The kayak had to be rolled over to drag my dead legs from it. I pulled my legs out, my hands digging up fistfuls of grass and dirt. For a while then as I sat on the bank the only movement to make was rubbing the life into the flesh of my legs.

When the stinging ache from lack of blood retreated, the next task involved restrapping the kayak to the car roof. The grass didn't make the haul up the bank to the car any easier. It caused me to slip and drop the kayak, smashing my hand between it and the dirt.

After hoisting the fiberglass shell onto the roof, the kayak strapped easy to the car. As I pulled down the straps tight a dull buzzing hummed through the area behind my eyes, not excruciating but building to it. Another turn of the crank. I got in my car, pulling the switch for the headlights then backing away from the river.

The lights cut down the cottonwoods until they lit up the way on the path to the bridge. The night was black and I wanted to sleep, but the only way to do that was to get away from there and go to Lincoln. At that moment I felt completely alone—lost without faith or family in the desolate Midwest.

Turning off the path onto the bridge, I slowed to see the moonlight reflect on the river in a sectioned beam of shimmering yellow light. The light came down the river in the shape of a triangle.

Looking down the road I drove on but I wasn't feeling good and as soon as I was out of the riverbed I felt *so* tired. It was crazy. I've never felt that tired in my whole life. I turned up the air conditioner and the radio as loud as I could stand. Air blowing into my face dried my eyes and they blinked to fight the air. The radio was static and the broken sentences of a talk show coming through on a shitty signal—I squeezed the steering wheel hard to feel the tension in my hands, squeezed it until my knuckles ached. Webbed blue veins on each forearm ribbed my skin.

I made it far like that, sitting on the edge of my seat, AC on high, the radio loud and a death grip on the wheel. At least a dozen miles. And I'm sure it was with that same posture that I fell asleep and hit the ditch.

A black sheet had been draped over my face and it didn't come off until my forehead hit the steering wheel. When sleep overtook me the car veered to the right, over the shoulder and into the bank of the ditch that ran along next to it, wedging dirt under the bumper and into the undercarriage. My car should have rolled, but instead it hit the facing bank and stopped.

The kayak didn't fare so well, though, it got launched what might have been fifty feet into the dried stalks of an unharvested cornfield, creating a tunnel that blocked it from view.

Shock and the stun from hitting my head kept me paralyzed in the car, staring into the space the kayak bored through the corn. My headache increased times ten.

After a minute I started the car, cranking hard on the ignition. But it was still wedged in the bank—it took rocking it back and forth many times before it came unstuck. After I got the car off the bank and pointed down the road, you would think my only problem then was how to get the kayak out of the field, but the weird thing was I didn't want it anymore.

Looking at the hole it made in the corn, how deep the tunnel was, and what just happened at the river made me think about it. It didn't take me very long to decide I didn't want to go drag it out of the field.

Pointed down the road, with a knotted forehead and open eyes I drove to Lincoln, wide awake, my headache growing more intense with each mile, one head light knocked out and empty kayak straps flapping in the wind. That line about boats against the current, born back ceaselessly. Fitzgerald, the hopeless, damned romantic, the best sentence writer of the Americans, the one that burned the closest to the flame, the beautiful, dream-ridden whimsy of a failed writer, who died believing it all used up and over, who went down further than most of us dare, who showed us the inside of the east egg then cracked apart. He wrote that, and I wrote it onto the cover of my notebook.

But it seemed a little slippery to be trying to remember at the time, with all the head trauma as it was, yet it was in moments like that that I relied on the teachings of the great writers the most, the old defenders of the human spirit, the old verities and truths of the heart. The light of the headlights reflected back to me. From the side of the road, down in the knee-high ditch weeds, two pair of yellowish-green eyes glowed in the night, not blinking, not moving.

At the corners of the county dirt roads, small green road signs shone when my headlights swept over them. The mile markers, white metal discs on the end of posts, sparkled like diamonds in the artificial light. Yellow dashes down the center of the highway appeared then passed-by on a conveyor. I was static, paralyzed, holding the wheel, the ground spinning the tires underneath.

Throughout the drive, throughout the slow cooling and deepening layers of thought as more of the ground rolled by, my mind returned to the lake, to the lawn around our house. It was always that way remembering a place, the images spun around, swirling in fleeting glimpses of different shades of color, some closer and more vivid, others less distinct and harder to see, and those were the ones, the ones way in the back, that I always tried to find. It bothered me some to think of all the lost memories, but by digging I could bring up an old image or even a story if I was lucky enough to grab hold with a strong hook.

The first one that came up I did not spend that much time with, I could easily and often revisit that place. It was a day on the lawn when I was eight. I found a snake, a thin green garter, and held it in my hands, watching it move, then let it move across my body slithering into my shirt and, as I drove down that dark highway, I could feel its cool scales on my skin. But that memory was not difficult enough, so I moved on, looking for one buried deeper.

Birds, turtles, shotguns, black dogs, fishing poles—all of them moved through my mind. Then a bigger one, a day, a longer moment, came to me. It was summer. I was twelve and old enough to take the four-wheeler from the yard. We owned a white, small cc machine that the twelve-year old me walked behind and pushed out of the yard, down the county road a hundred yards because Dad was sleeping, then started with the pull-start and got on. The noon sun the only thing in the sky, it burned down naked, and my arms could feel the heat warming tired muscles. Wind blew the water in my eyes to the corners, dragging the tears out and across my temples. Behind me, the quad kicked up a house-sized cloud of dust.

I drove until I stopped the four-wheeler at the creek at the bottom of the hill—pushing it to the side of the road at the end of the bridge, under a white Weight Limit 10 Tons sign. A small forest of cottonwood trees shaded the creek, a break from the sun. I went down to the edge of the creek and threw in a rock to watch it splash. Then I walked down the length of the bank, away from the bridge, down a hill deep into the cottonwoods. It was quiet and cool under the shade of the trees, the water bubbling with a small sound.

The hill sloped upward and I walked up and away from the water, through thicker cottonwoods. I was thinking about how I had better get back soon because he would be getting up from his nap and we were to finish putting the sharpened blades on the lawnmower. That was until I walked into a clearing of short green grass and weeds.

It was a small clearing, the size of a driveway, and at the end a plaid blanket lay on the grass. Curious, I walked over to the blanket and saw a pouch of tobacco and a leather water bottle lying at the top of the blanket. Crouching to see the bottle closer, I could smell the man who slept there but I didn't touch anything. I put my hands behind my back. Behind me the sun warmed the center of my back then spread out across my body. It was the hottest part of the day and sweat came through my pores.

I walked over to the end of the blanket to see what else I could find. A piece of paper stuck out from under the corner. Then a man came up behind me and—

"Hey boy, you get out of there!" he yelled.

I never saw the man and ran as fast as I could into the woods as his laughter thundered behind me. I ran into the trees, tripping over a stone, scratching my side on a branch, tearing my t-shirt, my lungs pumping, never looking behind me, gasping, my imagination contorting the face of the man into a steadily more menacing shape, the beard growing thicker and darker, his height rising higher, voice deeper, louder, closer. My shoulders waited to feel his hands grip them, the silence except for my feet and the branches I broke holding all the violence in the world.

When I came to my four-wheeler I fumbled with the pull-start rope, forgetting to put the machine into neutral first. It wouldn't start until I used the foot lever to get it into the right gear, then I pulled the rope twice before it started. I pushed the thumb throttle until my thumb burned from the pain of the pressure, turning around, watching the river for a man stumbling as he climbed up the bank, not yelling or screaming, just running faster than the small powered machine could carry me.

After a few hundred yards on the dirt road the cloud of dust behind the four-wheeler blocked the bridge, though every time

I looked back through the dust I thought I was going to see the man diving to grab the metal rack on the back of the machine and drag himself up. So I would turn my head around to the road in front of me, trying to forget the images my mind made.

When I made it home Dad was standing in the middle of the yard, waiting for me.

That was about all the juice the memory held and the yellow dots of the highway came back to me, or I came back to them, either way all the dots on the highway I passed could not make me feel any more awake.

17

When I awoke fully clothed under the sheets of my hotel bed, it was mid-afternoon on Wednesday and the meeting I was supposed to have with the dean was long since past. That was it for the University of Nebraska and that worried me for about one second. Focus shifted so fast the act of formulating guilt could not build a strong enough foundation to intrude into my thoughts and remain a problem. I rubbed my eyes, turning on the TV as I went in the bathroom to take a shower.

The noise of advertisements died when the bathroom door closed. I stumbled when I pulled my boxers off in the small space of the hotel bathroom, catching myself by landing my shoulder into the wall. My grace used up and gone.

With the spray on the back of my neck, I sang half finished lyrics under the weight of the water. The protest lyrics of a songwriter from Omaha, the unassumed voice of my generation. For a long time I stood with my eyes closed and the water hitting my neck until I turned and sat down in the tub, staring into the drain. Swirling, vague memories, short and long term, freely associated with other memories, linked and pulled themselves through my mind as a chain. I thought of taking baths as a kid when I was sick with chicken pox and how good the bath made me feel. I thought about the stage of the school where we performed for winter and spring concerts, the cardboard guitar that served as my prop when we were a rock band. Reaching that far back caused feelings of sadness so I pulled myself out of the tub and toweled off with wrinkled hands. The day was not old enough for all those memories.

The clothes I wore were the same I always wore. A black t-shirt and black jeans, but I sported the hat then and that went on as I walked out of the room and to the elevator and out of the hotel. The black soaked up the sunlight that poured over everything out in the afternoon day. Black the color that didn't make me feel obvious.

Out on the streets everything seemed to move slower, people tiring in the middle of the day. All the promise of a different day exposed as false, that day just the same as the last, the differences unnoticeable. My head felt better from sleeping but I was tired; I wanted some caffeine so, after a few blocks I spotted a coffee shop and went to get some soda.

Inside, the coffee shop held couches arranged in the front of two windows looking out to the street. Wooden, two-person tables filled the room up to the bar and pastry rack. Lincoln students studied with headphones on, drank coffee, played chess, and read.

After I got my soda I saw a kid over against a wall reading a book I read a little but never finished. It was good yet somehow I lost it. But I knew enough about it to go over and talk to him. It had been so long since I talked to anyone my own age.

"That's a cool book," I said.

He tipped it down and nodded. He looked normal enough. Short, brown hair and glasses. Clear blue eyes.

His book went up as my glass rested on the table. At first I didn't want to bother him—he was reading that important book and he turned sideways in his chair, crossing his legs. So I could tell he wanted to read more than he wanted to talk. Analyzing his behavior was an invasion and without anything to read on my own talking sufficed. I know how to be quiet and respect someone's space, but I wanted to talk to him; I wanted to know what or how he thought. There were times when curiosity could not be stifled and interrogation was an acceptable form of social interaction.

"What do you think?" I asked.

He tipped it down, looked at me, then set it down, took off his glasses, and rubbed his eyes. He looked at the table and you could tell he was searching for the right words, the best words.

"You have to realize that when he wrote this it was considered science fiction. Now it's considered literature." He looked up at me, then at the table as he continued. "This book is still relevant, and he wrote it a long, long time ago."

He shook his head a little then looked at me.

It was weird, I had read so much, read my entire life, but talking about it made me feel sort of like I was bragging, but different, so I dodged the question. Talking about books was something that made me uncomfortable, I didn't know where to start and what to say.

He carried the conversation.

"It's the one thing that resonates with me the most. It's not the most impressive sentence writing, but for some reason it hits me just right. And to me that's the important thing about books. That if you read them at the right time you can understand more about yourself from those pages then decades of living."

I'm not sure what he meant really, but I went along with it.

"Ethan Fulton," he said.

"Carrick," I said, and offered my hand. He gave me a weak handshake. He must not have shook hands very much.

He moved in his chair, and I knew I was getting too personal when he picked up his book and read again. The light of the interrogation chamber grew too bright. But I wanted to keep talking to him and I knew if he started in with the book I'd have to leave. There was a good way to play the conversation, but it wasn't the version we were playing.

Lipping the straw and drinking, the soda gave me energy but it also made me sick to my stomach, the sugar in my mouth coated and stuck to my teeth. Rubbing my tongue across my teeth confirmed it. I thought about how to regain his attention—once someone decides they will not participate, it is almost impossible to get them to change their mind. I took another drink of my soda, drinking until it made noise from the air between the straw and the bottom of the cup, which has to be one of the single most annoying sounds in the world.

When I set the cup down empty and reached for my backpack pain tore through the patch of brain directly behind my brow. It felt like someone took the bridge of my nose in a pair of pliers and squeezed with full strength. I gasped and winced, putting my hand up to my forehead, but that didn't help anything. The pain came from within.

After rubbing my head, my hand came down and Ethan looked at me.

"Are you all right?"

"Are there any parties tonight?" I asked.

Ethan wanted to pursue the first question, but my forced smile helped convince him the pain passed.

"My friend Lars has a house with a couple friends from my hometown and they party almost every night."

People and the thought of meeting new friends, friends that partied every night, sounded good.

"I don't know if they're doing anything, but they usually are, so I'll see. But I have to read this."

He tapped the ink-infused paper.

As I looked at my hands on the table my parents shot through my conscience and I developed a pressure on my chest. Not from missing them as much as thinking that the school called them and told them of my dishonorable discharge. I looked into the veins between my knuckles as the imagined voice of my father asked me what the hell I thought I was doing.

"You want to blow all your chances, don't you? You want to stay in Scottsbluff your whole life, do manual labor until you're too old to walk? Don't you? You must. If you don't go school then you must. I thought you

were smarter than that."

After he finished I sort of cleared my throat and made the arrangements with Ethan.

Shadows grew on the sidewalks outside. They formed in the corners where the buildings met the concrete then spread out black and wide until they covered the things that created them. Turning down the street, a gust of wind rattled the red windbreaker on the man I passed on the sidewalk. He nodded and said hello as he passed flapping.

I thought it would be a good idea to get a bottle for the party but I was sick of trying to find a buyer, finding some homeless or crazy person. I hated the way it made me feel. So instead I walked down the street in the darkening shadow and ended up at the old train station—a good choice for once.

The station hadn't run out of the middle of the city for decades, and the black steam engine they kept as a tourist photo-op hadn't run for a hundred years. But it didn't matter that the only use they knew for it was as a backdrop for pictures. History can be a valuable validator in even small doses. The train made me wish passenger trains were still operational, I would have taken one right then—rode it through the mountains to the ocean, stopping when the rail met the water.

As I spaced out looking at the train, I thought about the people I would meet on it: travelers, businessmen, families on vacation to visit an aunt, maybe in Florida or Arizona, a girl who just wanted to see the world. A girl who needed to have someone to be happy about as much as I did. A girl who could make living okay.

After that thought depressed me, then came the realization that the last thing I wanted to do was stand there staring at a train all day—it was making me sentimental and I hate that, so I wandered around Lincoln, telling myself not to stop and stare at anything, to keep walking, moving, until I returned to the coffee shop. If you don't stop then you don't have to think.

I walked all over downtown Lincoln, a city of average design. Most of the buildings were architecturally void of creativity, no embellishments with anything, strictly functional and strictly boring. One of the lone buildings with a fragment of character, the state capital building, proudly displayed a statue of a man in the act of throwing seeds from the top of a golden dome.

At the end of that street I passed a park where the father of two daughters sat on a park bench, watching his girls swing in sun dresses, pig tails floating up when they came down. He seemed sadder than you would think. Farther down, toward the edge of all the cool restaurants and shops, I saw an ambulance parked in front of a retirement home with its lights on and the back door open.

My heart longed for a real adventure to make it all mean something. It could have been a van of hippies stopped on the side of the road on their way to a commune, a girl in a convertible driving to California, an old man in an RV who just needed company. It didn't matter. All that mattered was that something happened to me, something real and defining and big and good. We all want it to be unique, to have meaning if not to the world then at least to us. My life must be original—it would not follow the footsteps tracked for years down through the generations in the same small, deeply rutted circle. There was more to life than tradition and conformity. My mind ran through all those thoughts as I walked down the sidewalks for what I guessed was an hour, before returning to the coffeehouse.

18

Ethan sat in the same spot. Against the wall, slouched down in his chair, holding the book vertical on the edge of the table. When he saw me he packed up and we left the coffeehouse. We got into his car parked at the meters on the street. He seemed smart and that meant something, and anyway it didn't matter, my whole philosophy was to keep myself as open as possible to whatever happened. The car was small like mine. He flipped on the headlights. The night set in and I felt okay.

He drove us through the open streets of Lincoln, two lanes and lined with houses, the lights on but the yards dark. The awkwardness of being in a car with a stranger. He played with the radio, turning the knob to try and find a station.

We drove under the passing lights in silence, making a few turns into a residential area, until we came to the house of Ethan's friends.

We parked on the side of the street behind a pickup, under a streetlight, and got out. The house I followed Ethan toward was a white, modest thing in a neighborhood of more of the same. A white sport utility vehicle with stickers on the back window sat in the driveway. As we walked up the concrete steps music and laughter came through the front door.

Ethan knocked twice as he opened it and the first thing I noticed when we walked in was the smoke—a thin cloud that slightly veiled the people sitting on a couch in the living room. It smelled sweet but also like stale ash.

Three guys sat playing video games, staring at the screen. This did not excite me for a number of reasons. Where there were video games there were never girls, and where there was pot smoke there was also only one type of girl—a type of girl that smiled too much, laughed too much, and never said much of anything. There was going to have to be a major change in events for an actual party to happen.

Only one of the guys on the couch acknowledged us when we came in, the other two were too enamored with the television.

"You guys doing this all night?" Ethan asked.

"All night," one of them said. "All day and all night. Railroaders do it all day and all night."

That one laughed hard but not as hard as the other two. They fell into each other and their faces turned red.

"We're like railroaders and shit," one of them said.

Ethan looked at me and matched the expression on my face with the tone of his voice.

"Let's go downstairs and get a beer."

He didn't talk as we went through the kitchen and down into an unfinished basement. Downstairs the walls were insulation and wood beams, the floor cement. Three naked light bulbs hung from the ceiling, giving the room more shadow than light. In the corner, two empty keg shells and one in a bucket of water stood next to an old sofa. Ethan went over to the one in the water and filled up two cups he found in a sleeve on the couch. The beer was warm and flat but I took a cup and drank. The alcohol still worked and I felt the headache turn. Ethan finished his beer then refilled the cup and went for the stairs.

We came into the kitchen and sat down at a small table in the corner. Ethan must have gotten a weird vibe from me then. He stood up from the table.

We walked into the living room and sat down on a love seat next to the couch. The three guys sat together, shoulder to shoulder, and they squinted to see the television. Staring seemed impolite but their fascination with the game interested me so my eyes traveled from each of them, to their vacant eyes, their hunched posture, and their tapping fingers. Most of the time there were no reactions. They mostly moved their hands and sometimes if it got difficult or exciting they would move their arms, but that was it. No change in the flat look in their eyes, no change in posture and barely any talking. Sometimes one would swear at the others, but mostly they just stared, and so did Ethan and I, until one of them got frustrated and handed Ethan his controller, which I thought he would laugh at. Instead he hit the buttons.

"What's with that hat?" the one who gave up said, not looking at me, watching the television. "What the hell kind of hat is that?"

He looked at me with a smile, a mocking look.

"It's just my hat."

"I know that. But what does it mean?"

"It doesn't mean anything. I got it from an old man at a sporting goods store."

"It's *sweet*," he said, laughing.

The rest of them couldn't think of anything else to do so they laughed. I sat back, turning my hat around and pulling it down. No one else talked to me or looked at me. They all sat staring straight into the box, their eyes boring hard, lapping up the images they were fed.

After a long silence, Ethan asked them who was coming over. One of them snorted, then, with a remote he found next to him, turned off the sound of the television and turned on some music. Music about doing the same drugs they were doing. But that didn't matter much, I sat there, not caring about what went on around me as they played silent. The only sounds were the music, the tapping buttons, and the noise of smoke moving through water. The cloud grew thicker and made it harder to see the other guys. I moved my right knee up and down.

For an hour the scene stayed the same, until a knock on the door and the sound of two girls laughing drove them into better posture. It was funny to see them react to the sound.

One of them put down his controller then switched off the game console on his way to the door. Another one opened a window then lit a candle. I would have known their names if they used them for each other but they hardly communicated the way it was, and after meeting the first one it didn't seem like asking them their names would have been much fun. They sat there staring at the blue screen for what must have been two minutes as the girls came in. Only when the voices of Sara and Sandra came close enough did they act as if they were doing anything. One lit a cigarette and the other changed the screen from blue to actual programming. The girls said hi then walked past them—the guys said hi as if coming out of a coma.

From the living room I could hear one of the two girls as she carried the conversation with striking confidence and clarity of voice. Her voice flew out of the kitchen articulate, succinct, and funny. She laughed at a joke she told and I found myself moving forward in my seat, then walking into the kitchen and standing at the corner of the counter—me and the two girls. She was still talking while she took a glass from the cupboard and I smiled at her story well before I understood the context. She filled the glass with water and when she finished talking I laughed. The other girl laughed the whole time.

She set the glass on the counter and made two quick steps, wiping her hand on her jeans before holding it out. I stepped forward and offered mine, changing my smile for a more earnest expression. I felt the need to impress her.

"Sara and Sandra. The S girls. S S. Secret Service Sara and Sandra," I said.

"Actually," Sara said, "we left our ear mics in the car. We're off-duty tonight."

"It's good to see the equal rights movement moving all the way up into the protection of the king," I said.

That was enough right then so I put my head down, sort of

looking at the tops of my shoes, then looked out into the living room. The smoke cleared a little and one of the guys slumped over on the sofa into an empty spot, almost asleep. The other one sat on the sofa with crossed legs and a cigarette.

Right then, all at once, standing there in that kitchen, I wanted to leave real quick, to walk out of that house and out in the streets. My neck craned to check the door, to see if it was open. It was closed but I imagined I could grab Sara's hand and take her out of there; I wanted to ask her if she owned a car and if we could drive away. The beer was in the basement but that was a place to rot, not a place to live. I thought Sara and I could do better—find a better way to die.

A hole opened up in the floor and the ocean and the sound of the waves, the sunshine and the sand spread out across the tile floor. All we needed to do to get to California was jump through the hole. But, like the blinking of an eye, the opportunity was lost, the hole closed up as fast as it opened.

I was staring at Sara's feet while she talked when the front door exploded in splinters and shards of flying glass. In the wreckage stood Lars, holding up a white paper bag, shaking it. He stood in the doorway in a perfect dramatic entrance. Lars was a big guy, long red hair, no neck, a football player type. A lineman. He stood there, shaking the bag, smiling, then he started dancing and singing. We all watched in silence.

"Daddy's got happy pills!" he yelled more than sung.

He did a ballerina spin and his body rippled when he came at us shaking the bag over his head. His feet were way more agile than you would expect for a man his size, but still the whole house shook. He spun into the center of the kitchen, rattling the bag in front of me, then Sara—moving down the line of us. We were all laughing at the ridiculousness. Lars's face was getting red and beads of sweat ran down the back of his neck into the spot between his shoulder blades. It seemed impossible for one person to make so much noise. He went into the living room, singing and shaking the bag and the kitchen laughed louder.

After the dance ended in the living room, Lars went for a beer in the fridge and with labored breath he told us how he found a new doctor to write a full prescription with two refills, and Ethan gave a cheers to Sara, who tucked her hands under her arms. Ethan held his unmet glass up for a second, said okay, then took a drink.

Lars looked at Sara, snorted, then walked out, with Ethan following, to the living room. We all followed far enough to watch Lars take the orange plastic bottle from his bag and spill the contents onto the coffee table. White pills spread out evenly on the wooden surface.

I found myself looking at my shoes. They were dirt stained from the river and the white caps on the toes were almost all brown. I noticed on the sides there was crusted dirt and green spots that reminded me of grass stains—the knees of my jeans in the spring and fall used to always be that color. Sometimes we would slide in the grass to see who could get the best grass stain, and thinking that made me smile.

After that thought my expression changed. I lifted my eyes and watched Sara and Sandra walk into the living room. It seemed a slight betrayal as I watched Sandra smile and tuck her hair behind her ear then sit down in between Lars and one of them. I wondered what would make her want to go toward something like that. Then Lars handed her the straw and as she took it, in one motion, eyes on the table, she sat forward and snorted lengthwise down the wood.

Sara didn't sit down, but stood watching at the end of the couch and I guess I just stood there watching Sara watch them. Still thinking about why they wanted to do this or be part of it. The pills on the table were unknown to me but if they were unfamiliar that meant they were not anything that needed to be known.

As time went on, the more they did it the more they talked, especially the two other guys—it seemed each time they ran the straw down the table was worth ten sentences and two smiles. Their voices rose and the laughter grew. Lars shook the rest of the bottle onto the table and one of them whistled.

"There's always more doctors," he said. "Oh doctor, I can't deal with it. C'mon doctor, it's too hard. C'mon doc, I've tried everything."

Lars laughed, looking around the room. They smiled but no one held his gaze. Sara sighed as she sat cross-legged on the floor next to the table, then fluffed up the back of her short brown hair with her hand, looking at the floor. If telepathy existed she would have taken my hand and gone to her car right then and driven us the two thousand miles to the ocean.

Ethan and Lars and their friends were getting along good, moving together in the same rhythm, going about their business as a group whose members all knew the rules and proper behavior. All except for Sara. She wasn't an honorary member nor did she care to be in the club; she looked as if she wanted to be anywhere but there. Watching her, thinking about the shame it was she was not somewhere better, where people took better care of people, I could feel the rush coming.

My eyes sunk and throat tightened and I knew I wasn't going to sleep that night. Tension pulled my skin taut, exposed nerves shot to the surface against their will, waiting to be scraped raw.

Silence created the first conflict when the CD ended and the music on the stereo died, the humming in my ears, the tape hiss, grew louder. The talking and performing never stopped, no one noticed—everyone fell in love with themselves for the first time. They all talked over and on top of one another, everyone the center of their own attention.

Sara shifted her weight off of her feet and sat up, straightening her back.

"Hey, do you guys know who you're going to vote for?"

As she was punctuating her statement with inflection one of the guys hit play on the music and everyone sat back and smiled as Sara asked the question. They stopped looking at her when her face turned straight and somber. She turned her head down, making me want to hug her or put my hand on hers.

That wasn't happening so I walked out to the kitchen to get another beer. Before leaving the living room I waited, watching her until she looked up at me, then I walked out, hoping she would follow. But she must have stayed there with the music on, looking at the floor as I went downstairs to the basement. Down to the dark basement with three naked light bulbs, a sofa by the keg. It was lonely and suffocating, dark and the air was hard to breathe.

In a spot like that she needed someone to take her out of that environment—someone strong and chivalrous and dashing. Someone to save her. But instead of running up and kneeling in front of her with a rose in my teeth, I got as much out of that stale keg as I possibly could. That seemed a more honest pursuit.

The beer was awful but I drank it anyway. As it took effect the alcohol cut away feeling, separating me from my senses. The voices upstairs got far away, quieter, and the rest of the atmosphere detached as if my sight, hearing, and thinking somehow withdrew into the recesses of myself. A mosquito fluttered around the naked light bulb overhead.

My plan was to get drunk sitting down there in that unfinished basement. But the alcohol only took my senses out of the environment; it didn't take me out of reality. The couch under me and walls surrounding me, the light above me and the cup in my hand, it all was there and real. I drank until my stomach hurt. It seemed to help the headache though it didn't really; it just dulled the squeezing band of metal around my head.

But alone and without the pressure of being around strangers, it felt good down there and better when the sounds coming down the stairs turned out to be the footsteps of Sara. She needed an out just as badly.

When she came in the room she was looking at her feet. She stopped when she realized she wasn't alone.

"This party doesn't have anything to do with me," I said.

She sat at the other end of the couch and tucked her feet underneath her.

"There are a thousand places I'd rather be, a thousand things that we could be doing," I said.

"Name one."

"Skydiving at night over the ocean."

"Good call. Maybe we should take over. This operation needs new leadership."

It seemed the right thing to do to encourage her to talk about anything she wanted. She glanced over at me and looked down into the couch.

I sat for a second, thinking, thinking about all the memories that floated at will through the middle section of my mind. Stories grew from these and if one would stick the story would come, all it took was for the memory to play itself out instead of the usual floating by as a Polaroid, allowing a brief glimpse but not moving, not rolling in action. Yet searching led to only fleeting images and the slide show was the sole entertainment provided at the moment. The panic that memory might fail came on, my mind gearing to switch to an excuse, but before it could fully switch over, under the pressure something came to the surface.

"My earliest childhood memory, or at least the one I think is my earliest, is from some holiday at a relative's house. I think it's my great-grandmother's but I'm not sure. That part's not clear.

"Anyway, I go down into the basement, this dark, dusty old basement and I can hear the sounds of the older people above me laughing. Like they're all sitting around a table playing a board game. In the memory I'm not sure what I'm doing, or what I'm looking for, I'm just looking around. So I come up to these statues, figurines, on a counter against the wall. There's so many, tons of these, I guess, porcelain, like two-inch tall figures. And they're all angels in an extended nativity scene—that's why I think it's Christmas. There's like two hundred of them. And I'm little, maybe six, and I'm about eye level or lower than the counter or table or whatever it is. Anyway, I take one of the angels down, hold it in my hand, looking at it. I turn it over in my hands for a little while then I start bending the wire of the halo back and forth, bending it in the same spot with my little fingers until it comes off in my hand. Then, when the ring breaks off, that's when the memory stops."

My leg came down from the couch and Sara stared at me.

"Now you have to go."

She straightened herself a little, pulled her feet closer to her.

"I don't know if this is my earliest memory, but my brother locked me in the trunk of a car and left me in there for a long time once. I almost died."

Sara looked down. It wasn't the best, most detailed story, and we stared at the wall for a second. The mosquito circled the light bulb.

"Oh, I think I've got an earlier one," she said. She looked over and smiled at me. "I can remember this one time my sister taking me on a horse across a hay field and I sat in front of her, holding onto the saddle horn. It seems like it would have been dangerous though if that's my earliest memory. And in it we were going like a hundred miles an hour."

She smiled and ran her hand along her thigh.

"Do you have any horses?" I asked. "Are you a cowgirl?"

"Two and yes, but you'd never know it. I don't throw my boots on too much."

"Horseback riding sounds fun."

"They're in Omaha. I'd like to see you ride horses in those shoes."

She pointed at my feet and laughed a little.

"I can ride like the wind."

"I bet you can."

"No seriously. Horses love me."

"I bet."

"They do. I always feed 'em carrots and pet their necks. I pet their necks and don't spur 'em hard."

My heels came together in front of me.

"You're not coming anywhere near my horses."

"Well if we can't ride horses we should ride each other."

She smiled at me, waiting for my explanation. But she didn't wait long.

"Oh my god! Did you just *say* that?"

I should have laughed it off, but instead I looked right at her.

"Are you serious?"

I kind of half smiled and looked at her, but she was getting uncomfortable then and holding her laughter.

"You *are* serious. Oh god. I have to go. This is hilarious."

She got up and walked up the stairs fast, taking the soul of me with her. Deflated, I decided the best thing would be to get another beer. It was the *only* thing to do. So I stayed down in the basement, watching the mosquito, sipping the stale liquid. I was filling up my cup when I heard the eruption of laughter. Sara, more than happy to go report the contents of our conversation, opened up a wound that gaped raw and sensitive, exposed nerves and torn skin. I thought about how many beers it would take until the gash closed or I passed out on that couch. People love to betray you, to expose you, as if they were doing you a favor by not being sensitive or gracious. More than anything, I was disappointed. Sara seemed better than that at first, a girl that wouldn't sell me out.

As I drank and thought about her, every word of our conversation running through me, it was almost as if my temperature rose two degrees each time I lifted my cup to take a sip.

Sweat pooled around my collar by the time Ethan came down. He stopped at the foot of the stairs. My cup touched my lips.

"Let's go. I've got class in the morning," he said.

As we went up stairs I focused on the pattern of the carpet under the soles of Ethan's stepping shoes. Alcohol swirled through my vision, forcing me to concentrate on the act of walking. My steps slowed when entering the kitchen, knowing what waited for me when we came to them.

The world snickered, shaking its head when I came through the living room, not stopping as we went for the door. They paused the music as we moved past the back of the couch, Ethan slowing down but my gait staying the same, and before we got to the door Lars called out.

"And they're off! And away they go! Hope you two aren't ridin' bareback!"

Ethan smiled a little, looking at me as he shut the door on a laughing house. We were silent as I followed him to the sidewalk, got in the car, waited while he started it, and watched him sit rigid as we drove off. Uncomfortable, from his silence and from my insecurity at having mixed, unclear emotions, it was hard to decide if it was my fault, if I messed the situation up, embarrassed Ethan, or Sara and Lars and his friends were petty and mean. Blaming myself was more my style.

19

Ethan looked at me out of the corner of his eye and turned up the radio, as if that was punctuation for the conversation. My head turned to the window and streetlights spreading out yellow light in circles on the road as we passed under green stoplights. Neither of us spoke as we drove along the road under the artificial lights, under the power lines, past the homes and the buildings, driving toward the place where we met. My thoughts remained on Sara and my hands clenched and relaxed as our conservation replayed over and over in my mind. Excuses for her lack of sensitivity surfaced and were buried, rising and falling, until the idea that she took the bad time she was having at the party out on me, entertained herself by making me feel bad. It didn't make me feel any better, but the understanding helped a little.

Still sitting rigid and silent, Ethan slowed in front of the coffeehouse, but my thoughts were stuck on recreating better questions to ask Sara.

"Do you live close?" he asked.

"I don't live anywhere around here," I said, "and my car's in a parking lot down the road. I'll sleep in it."

The plastic of the door handle felt cheap and brittle in my hand.

"You're going to stay in your car?"

Wind helped the door open and I held the door from springing.

"Get in. You're not sleeping in your car."

Ethan looked at his watch, sighing in a bothered way, and I

shut the door. He didn't speak again until we parked diagonally in front of his apartment building. We got out of the car and went inside, up the elevator, still not talking, still standing as far away from one another as possible. He felt obligated then, as if he was doing me a favor. It was no longer a positive choice. He felt as if taking care of me was his duty and my resentment grew.

After showing me the couch and throwing down a pillow and a blanket, he stood in his bedroom doorway with the light from his room casting a shadow over him. He looked at his shoes as he handed me a blanket.

The cat hair coated blanket caused immediate sneezing, my neck and face popping up hives so I threw it to the floor. After that there was no chance of sleeping, my nose running, my throat swelling up. I went into the kitchen to get a glass of water and a paper towel. The coffee cup said "World's Number #1 Dad." There weren't any paper towels so I blew my nose with the towel on the stove. Then, in a sudden pang, hunger struck hard, and I went for the fridge, replaying the words Ethan last spoke.

In the white vertical box was a carton of eggs and one of milk. I took them out and set them on the counter. Under the stove was a skillet, which went on the stove that heated it. The white eggs cracked against the silver rim, four of them, and the added milk swirled in the yolks.

As they heated I looked for a fork to stir them and chop up the yolks. I opened a drawer and instead found a pile of pictures with faces next to smiling faces. Standing there, swirling through the pictures I thought about all the people I knew in my life, how they all leave as soon as they come, how they all disappear and reappear, most of them forgetting about you, never telling people that they even knew you. I looked at those pictures, some of Ethan with the people from the party, and how they would all end up alone anyway, and I wondered why they even did it, why they even let themselves know each other, make those connections, but then I thought about how that *was* what it was, that's *why* we did it. But then I thought that wasn't why. It was that we all wanted to feel good—and other people could do that. The eggs heated behind me and I found a picture of Sara and Ethan backdropped by mountains.

They wore beanies and held skis in their hands, happy, smiling with red cheeks, close faced. I was sure they smiled when they saw that picture. It was a good one—one that you would smile each time you saw. One that would make you animate the memory, make it move, relive it, until you thought about where the other person was or what they were doing or who they were married to or where they lived or about the last story you heard about them. Then you would stop, put the picture down, look at it one last time before shutting the drawer.

But for me, looking at that picture, I wanted to be in that scene so bad that I imagined that I was the one taking the picture. That I took a picture of them and then they each got in a picture with me. That after that we all got on the ski lift, went to the top, hooked our skis in, and glided down a full-on fresh powder run, the sunlight at our backs, a light snow falling, me following Sara, Ethan following me, making long, lazy turns in the ankle-deep powder, smiling and laughing.

That's what I was thinking about when Ethan came out of his room—just as I noticed the smoke from the burning eggs behind me. I folded the picture in half, tore it down the middle and put the half of Sara in my pocket. I went for the door and out the hall as Ethan stuck his head out.

"You loser!"

I would remember those words for a long time, the way he said them with so much disgust and malice.

When I returned to the hotel I checked to see if I still had a room. They said I did and that there was a message for me, that my mother called. That news caused all the nerves in my body to shoot out of my skin, exposed and tingling. There was nothing I could tell them that would make it any better. It was too late for the university. To them, I ruined my best shot at a good career.

My parents no doubt were trying to get a hold of me for days, calling every number they could, and since my cell phone was at the bottom of the canal, they were even more concerned. All that and the thought of how worried my mother was made me feel terrible. I never could just shrug off making my mother worry. Thinking about her not sleeping, or going to work worried, made me sick.

From the phone in my room I called a limousine before I checked out of the hotel. I figured I should exercise what remaining freedom I still possessed, do something fun before the sky started on fire. I walked out front and sat on the curb until the long black car came to the front of the building and a woman with red hair in a black pant-suit stepped out and opened the door.

As I adjusted to the interior, the glass, leather and lights, the plexiglass divider rolled down and she asked me where we were going.

"Yeah, sure, the ATO fraternity. Do you know where that is?"

She whirred up the divider and I looked in the refrigerator for some champagne, found a bottle of brown liquor instead and poured myself a glass on the rocks. It was terrible and I tried to drink some but it was disgusting, tasted like cardboard. I sat there in the middle of that big limousine seat, thinking about all those frat brothers sprinting out the doors when they saw the limousine pulling up, how they would come running, smiling, tackling, pile in and one of them would know of a party anywhere, someplace where girls would be, someplace where people would know people like me. A place where I could get lost in a bathroom with a strange girl that knew what I wanted.

Streetlights and empty sidewalks were all I could see from the side windows. The red taillights of a passing car reminded me of the clock at the hotel and I remembered the doll on the nightstand. The unblinking, painted blue eyes. How rigid and brave she sat.

I tried to drink the glass of bourbon but it made my nose burn, so then I tried to get excited about seeing all those guys I never had a chance to meet. All the guys that would take me sailing later in life. I knew they would be up partying, hanging out of the windows, throwing beer cans.

We weren't far from the frat when we left the hotel, so it didn't take too long before we stopped out front. Before I could even drink half of the glass the driver came around and opened my door.

The frat was dark and quiet, not what I expected. I stayed inside the car, waiting for them to come running out. The driver got behind the wheel and before she rolled up the plexiglass she said she needed to get going.

"Can you hold on? I'm sure the guys are coming out. They're on their way. Just wait a sec."

We waited for a while then, long enough for me to sip down the glass of bourbon, but no one came. So I had her drive over to the green lot, the ride short and blurry, and she let me out in the middle of the lot. I paid and thanked her. Standing in the middle of car rows with early morning dew forming on the windshields, looking around for my car, for anything, for my one true love. I thought it too late to be looking for a person, but I still went toward the apartment where I met Carmen. If anyone could help it was the prettiest girl in the last couple of days. She seemed to have her head organized well enough to let me hold on, to let me grab a pole as the tornado passed. It wasn't that far and the way was still fresh.

Walking as the night deepened cold and dark my black t-shirt felt thin and insufficient. I walked across the north end of campus out of the lights of the school and into the streets of the neighborhoods. The birds were waking up, singing the forecasts. The late hour meant there were no parties to go to, even I knew enough to know that, but there had to be *somewhere* to go, somewhere where people were still alive. I thought when the sun rose I could see about getting an apartment in the complex, one next to Carmen's friends so that Carmen would knock on my door sometimes, tell me where the parties were, that she had broken up with her boyfriend, could she come in?

"Sure. Sure Carmen, come in."

"You don't mind? You sure? No, I should go."

"No no stay, you can stay in my bed. I'll sleep on the couch."

The smile she gave walked with me past the white houses set back on green lawns, past the mailboxes at the end of concrete walkways, until I came to the building maze apartment complex.

Aside from the voices of the birds and the legs on my body no one moved under the lifting night. But since the destination was programmed into my mind miles ago my legs went up the steps to the friend of Carmen's, to the front door, which opened when the handle was turned into the black apartment. The blackness made it impossible to breathe. The sound of everything amplified. Even when I backed-out and left and the door closed quietly behind me, a small click, the sound shot electrified wires through my ears.

Stepping softly down the wooden steps, I walked over to the clubhouse front office. It was closed. Laying down with my head on my bag, I fell asleep as the sun rose in the east.

20

The same sun came a long way before it woke me with a sharp light directly overhead. Around me most of the cars that parked in front of the buildings were gone. My head throbbed and I pulled my hat down before standing up. When I did stand it took a second to understand what walking meant, how it was performed.

After a reassessment, I walked away from the apartment complex and, from the heat that arose through the ground into me, it seemed the earth moved closer to the sun with each step. The idea of the university grew stale and my feet led me away from it. It didn't take many steps of rubber on sidewalk before my body became sick with walking in the heat.

The college and the apartment complex shrank away and when I came to the interstate I walked under the bridge—the shadow over the sidewalk cooled the air so I slowed. The air didn't move much, the difference in temperature immediate, and it felt as if, by the sun being blocked, my body let out a sigh. A voice ran down the slope to meet me.

A man in the corner, at the point of the wedge under the bridge, rasped down at me.

"Hey son. Hold on a second," he said, his voice grating at his throat.

I moved to the center of the road.

"Son. Hold on. I'm not going to hurt you or nothin'. Just hold on."

The man stumbled when he came down the hill but he didn't ask for money.

"Hey. Son. Hold. Hold on. Hold on a second now." The sound of rolling pebbles followed his steps. He walked up close to me wearing a bright orange stocking cap, a flannel shirt, and tan work boots. If we were in the north he would have been a lumberjack. He smelled, wheezing when he breathed. He wanted a lot of things, for sure, but what it was possible to give him was different. He tried to smile but his cracked lips couldn't stretch that far.

"You got any smokes?"

My pocket held four. I removed two and held them out. He took the cigarettes out of my hand and went up the hill, out of the wind. When he came down he held two lit cigarettes and handed one to me. I took it and ripped off the filter, throwing it far enough away from us so that he wouldn't chase after it.

I looked at him, at his lips, then I looked down.

"No bum lips, today?" he asked. He laughed a big, throaty laugh, putting his shoulders back to bellow out. But the big thing got caught in his throat and he bent over, coughing. I felt like leaving right then but I didn't know if I could, if I could turn my back on something as sad as that. I wanted to pat his back but he recovered.

I stayed to finish the cigarette, though I wasn't sure I was helping him any.

He offered me one of the hands he just coughed all over. Before I took it I looked at it for a second.

"Name's Jack. What's a matter? You don't shake hands?"

"No, no, I do," I said, and shook it. It was rough and strong. "So is this where you live?" I asked, gesturing at the underbelly of the bridge.

"Got laid off. Need shelter, have to survive somehow, y'know? I'm looking for a job."

Jack stood straighter and looked down the sidewalk out from under the bridge. I didn't know what to say. It was uncomfortable and the heat returned; I was getting sick just standing there, looking at my feet. Anywhere would have been better than that right then—I wanted to help him but I had no idea how. The silence lasted until Jack rumbled his throat.

"Thanks for the smoke, kid. Hey I got this can of pickles?"

The heat level increased and I pushed my hands deeper into my pockets, trying to breathe. The last thing I wanted to tell him was it was a jar, but the thought came to me anyway. Jack ran up to his bed at the wedge of the bank and bridge, and rummaged in his stuff, pulling blankets apart, wrecking his bed.

"I have to go Jack. It was nice to meet you," I said. "Good luck."

That also made me feel terrible. Jack stopped what he was doing to watch me leave. I walked out into the sunshine, turning once to make sure Jack was not following, then away from the sound of the cars over the interstate, the low hum and the rushing wind. I left the bridge with the smell of Jack in my nostrils and the sound of his coughing in my ears.

When I was far enough away I kept thinking about living off pickles. After walking for a block or so, I remembered there was a liquor store down the street—the one I went to with Kathy.

It seemed as good of a place as any so I went over there and went in. I walked around dazed by the artificial lighting, sizing up the store clerk.

From the refrigerator I took out a bottle of milk, a bottle of water and a bottle of orange juice. They were all I could carry and I took them up to the counter then went to the side counter. I grabbed a stick of deodorant, a tube of toothpaste, a bottle of shaving cream, a package of disposable razors—I wasn't sure if that was a good idea but I figured he would have to try hard to hurt himself with the pink, plastic things—and took those up to the counter. He still needed food and there was some room in my bag plus what I could carry, so I got a bag of pretzels, apples, oranges, and a banana. I thought he could use some gum and I also got him three sandwiches. The clerk put everything in plastic bags, rang it up, and I charged it to my credit card.

The plastic handles dug into my hands and the bags caught my legs as I walked everything to the bridge. When I got there Jack's stuff was still in the same place but I didn't see him around—I thought maybe he was under his bedding, but nothing happened when I nudged it with my foot. I called out but got no response, figuring since he left all his stuff he would be coming back, so I set everything next to his bed and put some of his blankets on it. That way no one else would get it. I called out one more time then walked away.

I turned around after a few steps to check and I thought I could see someone moving under the bridge next to the stuff, but the sun made it hard to see in the shadows and I wasn't sure if it was him.

Jack's lips cracking open with a smile but then switching to determined hoarding floated in front of me as I walked to the hotel feeling better. I should have been happier for him but I kept thinking about him doubling over and coughing and his lips cracking. The sound of him coughing under that bridge, rolling around as he tried to fall asleep, made me sad. Then I thought about myself, what the hell I was doing. That was a hard subject to grasp.

Lost in thought, I stumbled in a daze through the brick industrial buildings. I could have been spinning in circles as much as the landscaped swirled. Of all the things that ran across my vision, the thought of Jack opening his jar of pickles bothered me the most. You know when you see those people sometimes and you think you might take his place under that bridge when he is gone, maybe you'll even join him while he's there, sleep across from him, on the other side. You straighten your posture, think about the clothes you have on, your last five decisions, how you spent the last week. That was where I was, walking to the hotel thinking about that bridge, the jar of pickles and Jack's bed, which led me to think of my bed at my parents' house. The bed that I would have kissed Jack on the mouth to sleep in. But before I could make my escape, my return home in a wisely played admitted defeat, I needed to get my car which required going to my room at the hotel and getting my keys.

21

At the hotel I walked through the front doors, past the front lobby to my room. The lights and television were on but the shades were pulled. My keys lay next to the doll on the nightstand.

When I went out to the parking lot to my car and tried the key it would not turn in the door. It was not my car. So I walked up the rows, looking but my car was not on that side, which seemed impossible.

I went through the hotel to the other side and checked that parking lot. I walked up that row and it wasn't there, so I went around back to look, and, not finding it, I went to the car that looked like mine and tried the key again. It still wasn't mine.

Thinking about where it could be, if it was stolen or parked anywhere else, I sat down on the concrete with my back to the trunk. It was not at the college I didn't think. It was stolen, had to have been. I went into the front lobby to call the police..

"Your car was towed," the bellboy said. "You left it in a handicap zone. I'll call you a cab to take you to the towing company. It should be out front in ten minutes. You can wait outside."

After a few minutes of waiting by the curb, the taxi stopped out front and I got in.

"Where ya headed?"

The black man wore a camouflage hat and sported a gray and white beard.

"California."

I slid down in my seat.

"California street?"

"No. Hollywood. Hollywood, California."

"Sorry. You've got the wrong airline. You want American."

The scenery swept by blurred in blobs of fingerpainted color. I'm not sure what I wanted to ask the cab driver. I think it was something about sex but I couldn't articulate it so it got quiet in the cab. Only the noise of the wind on the windows. It would get louder when the wind would pick up, but most of the drive was the sound of the wind on the windows and the motor noise. We drove on in silence until we got to the car lot. I could not ask him what I wanted, could not explain myself. But that wasn't uncommon to me anymore, my tongue wrapped itself around the stem of my brain and they were not friends.

The car lot was surrounded by chain-link fence. As we approached, I saw a silver pickup truck that sent fear through my body—much too familiar.

The taxi stopped in front of the gates behind a police car.

"Here we are. Universal Studios."

I slapped a twenty on the man's shoulder and slid out of the seat. I shouldered my bags and took out my keys. The cop car was parked at an angle in front of the office booth—I walked past it, through the chain-link fence toward the window of the office. The officer stood talking to the clerk, but when I looked out at the cars in the lot I stopped.

My car pulled out of the spot it was parked in a small distance down the row of other cars. I dropped my bag and looked at the silver pickup and checked the county of the plates. 21. Scottsbluff county. The police officer who stood in front of the booth took a picture from his chest pocket, looked at it, then looked at me. I watched my car come closer toward us as the police officer walked at me and my car stopped in front of my feet. I looked through the car window at the face of my father.

He threw open the door and charged at me. Before I could react—

"You're done. You're going home right now. All the fun's over.

You blew it."

My mother came out of the ticket clerk's office, a pale look on her face. She stopped and looked at me then at my father, who stood one foot in front of me.

Later, they told me the bank called to alert my parents I overdrew my account. They wanted to make sure someone had not stolen my credit card. After calling hotel to hotel in the Lincoln phonebook, they found where I was staying but could not reach me, so they filed a missing person's report then got in the truck and came to Lincoln.

They were ten miles out of town when the towing company called about my car. They came straight there to get it before it was impounded.

He still stood inches from me.

"What the hell is the matter with you?" he asked. "You don't take the chances that were given to you?"

The police officer stepped in then and took me to his car and asked me a few questions. We went to the car where he asked me what I'd been doing. I failed to explain myself.

SCOTTSBLUFF II

22

Mom waited in the lobby of Dr. Kennard's office for me and stood when I came out. My gracious and wonderful mother who never judged but only sought understanding, eternally patient and forgiving. It was reliving the memory of the nightmarish days and nights in Lincoln that provided my catharsis, and, though my understanding was less than complete, I felt my burden lifting.

We walked to the car without talking, got in, then drove away in silence. A line of immigrants stood on the sidewalk in front of a convenience store, waiting to be picked up by farmers or anyone else who needed cheap labor.

We came up to an empty intersection and a red stoplight. She slowed down and applied the brakes to stop. When she did the car went into a full slide, rotating to the left to slide through the intersection broadside and stop when the front, right side hit the median. She pushed the gearshift up to reverse and straightened the car out then started down the road. Her hands gripped tight on the steering wheel and her eyes on the ice.

We set a course for the last grocery and department store, the last car dealership, the last nursery, the last place to buy anything with a shopping cart in Scottsbluff. Once the supercenter was built the town grew around the store—actually the town didn't grow, it shrank, but the survivors all moved closer to the town's central organ, the streets built off of it, branching out like arteries, the driveways the valves. As we drove into the parking lot I swore I saw the walls pulsing.

We entered the automatic doors of the supercenter. The cholesterol and fat, the artery clogging substances of the heart of a 400-pound, short, middle-aged woman, spread out before us, aisle after aisle. Kennard's voice echoed in the soundspace of my mind. The comforting thought of attempted continuous honesty, a way to begin again.

We walked through the aisles toward the shoe racks. At the display rack for discounted fertilizer a farmer and his wife stopped us.

"Hey Cheryl, hey Carrick," he said. "Would you guys mind telling that wind to stop blowing?"

"That would be nice wouldn't it?" Mom said.

On we walked to the shoes.

"Carrick?"

I turned around to the smile of Sasha Mason, an old classmate.

"Hey, Sasha," I said.

I panned the signs above the aisles. Food. Linens. Hardware. Sporting Goods. No Exit.

"Hey, I don't know if you heard, but we're all going over to Kendra's tomorrow night. I mean like everybody that's in town is going. It should be pretty fun. You should come."

She smiled. I looked through her.

"Okay, bye, Carrick," she said, almost as a question.

"What do you think?" Mom asked. "Should we get your father these?"

She handed me a box of work boots to carry. On the way to the food section Mom saw someone she knew looking at the kitchenware.

"Carrick! I heard you were in town. How's school?"

A cowboy threw a lasso over my head and the slipknot slid tight around my neck. My mother's friend squeezed my arm and I jerked before I could think. The cowboy took the rope-end and walked to his buckskin horse.

"Don't you just love running into all these people you know?" Mom said. "Here it is. We need two loaves of white. And get the sale kind."

I took the bread from the stand. The palms of my hands were sweating so I held it by the ties. The cowboy began wrapping the rope around the saddle horn in slow, deliberate movements, looking at me. We went to the deli and ordered a twelve-piece, half crispy, half original bucket of chicken. Each wrap took up more slack from the rope.

"Darn it. I wanted to get you some new jeans. Here. If we go over there now and hurry the chicken won't get too cold."

She walked fast over to the sale rack in the men's section.

"What size are you? 30? Here's two. Go try these on. Here, I'll take that, or you can just set it down."

"Carrick? Hey!"

The cowboy mounted the horse. I knew that voice. I clenched the jeans in my fists.

"Hey! What are you doing here?! Looks like you're getting hooked up with some new clothes. Hittin' Mom up for some jeans?"

The cowboy spurred the buckskin and it took off in full gallop.

She waved at my Mom, who waved back and smiled, then acted like she was interested in the men's coats, leaving us to talk. "How have you been?!" Maribel asked me. "I'm so glad I got to see you!""

The rope went taut.

"Look, we've got...I need to try these on." I held up the jeans. "I mean, we've got chicken?"

"Okay. Call me sometime."

I took the jeans to the slotted door of a dressing room, shutting the door and hanging them on the wall. Then I saw myself in the calming effect of the reflective glass. His eyes met mine and I sat back on the bench. How could she have been there?

Why would she come up to me with that good mood, that smile? How the hell could she be so *healthy*? As if nothing bothered her about seeing me. What did she think of our relationship to come up to me and act so damn *healthy*? I leaned up against the corner and watched my shoes stay on my feet. The resolution became to never leave the dressing room. I was a discriminating shopper. I was taking my time making my decision. I was incapable of performing any action. Jesus. Maribel Carter with supercenter jeans in my hands and the way I couldn't talk. I reached up and loosened the elastic of my shirt collar.

I took the jeans down off the wall and pulled off my shoes and walked around in the room in case she was watching, but I didn't take my jeans off. There wasn't any point. I slid my shoes back on and walked out with the jeans.

"They didn't fit."

She handed me the chicken and we went to stand in line at the register. Magazines with celebrities without makeup and messed-up hair watched us move toward the cashier. We paid and bought a book of American flag stamps. The bagger put the boots in one white plastic bag and the bread and chicken in another and handed them to me. I could see through the windows a white storm of snow falling on the cars in the stretching parking lot—the wind was dead and the sky a thick, low-lying gray. The cashier counted out the change and I turned toward the door with our bags. The snow fell in dime-sized flakes, covering our heads and shoulders in the short walk to the car.

Dark tire marks striped the white highway as we drove home slow with the food. The car door had severed the cowboy's lasso and I could breathe again. Engine noise and the tires throwing slush against the undercarriage soothed my exposed and abraded nerves. All the gray and brown of the fields and plains was coated in white.

As we drove my thoughts went to Lincoln.

"You don't know anyone at this party do you?"

A balcony ledge and standing, looking across a parking lot, to my legs swinging over and falling off the dorm ledge.

Then the slide and a swirling mosaic of words written on the walls. The taste of vodka in my throat.

Falling asleep in the yellow kayak on the riverbank, waking up to the stars, falling asleep again on the way home, launching the kayak through the cornstalks.

The hat they laughed at at that guy's house, Lars. And Sara, the confident one. The one that betrayed my foolishness. The keg beer in the basement and all the white lines cut up on their table.

A blank blue television screen. The red hallway carpet. Wandering around parking lots.

I thought about that, ran my mind over it for some answer, for some type of help, and, as we drove along the striped, white highway, I went back again.

To all my silence and lack of self-respect. How I failed to stand up for myself. How I was just letting myself get swept along without making any smart moves or decent decisions. But I couldn't describe the thoughts I was having in a clear conclusion, or express them with any type of real insight. So we drove on in quiet, still silence, until we came to our frosted home.

Mom took the food in and I needed to be alone to consider the new thoughts I saw swim before my eyes. I wrapped my body in sweaters, scarves, and coats and went out to the dock. My boots compressed the snow with a wet crunching and I could feel the color of my ears and nose reddening.

Out on the dock, looking across to the puddle of a lake, the actual frozen water seemed manufactured, a piece of glass left behind, a mirage in the desert. Above it, and to the west, pink fingers, I counted eight, stretched across the sky, the thumbs of the two hands held under to spin the globe. The air cold, I stepped down from the dock and went to the shed.

The naked light bulb lit the shed in pale yellow. Again I went to the trunk and set the pheasant to the side. The painting felt lighter then the time Maribel and I looked at it together—when it showed us the brightest colors. I turned it around, expecting the colors to be different, maybe lighter shades, less vivid. But I didn't expect the complete change: the top block faded into frozen water blue and the bottom block into light yellowish gray.

The painting returned to the trunk. I went out of the shed to the center of the yard, holding my palms up to collect snowflakes. The snow came up over my boots and I fell back into it, onto the ground, staring at the sky. Above me, gray sky turned to black.

I stayed on my back, watching the sky turn black and yellow until I shook. Then I arose from the cold ground and joined them in the house for the chicken and after, hot chocolate. After we ate they turned the television on and I went to my room with a book. As I read the phone rang three times and each time I thought it would be Nate.

"Hey, so are you coming tomorrow night or what?"

"I don't think my car's going to make it in this snow."

"We'll come out and get you."

I set the book down and went out to the living room.

"Hey, if you guys don't mind, I'm going out tomorrow night."

"I don't know, Carrick," Mom said. "There's a lot of snow and they say there's more on the way."

"Nate's got a four-wheel drive truck."

"It *would* be good for you to get out of the house, go have some fun with your friends. We'll talk about it tomorrow."

I went to my room. This was good. I fell back on my bed. Maybe I should stop thinking about her. Before I fell asleep I checked the snow—it was still falling, making up for its lost time, an effort to stop the drought in one storm.

In the morning I awoke hours behind the sun. But the gray snow clouds covered it anyway, and I fought to leave the warmth of my bed for the cold air of the house. After breakfast I piled on snow gear to see the effect of the ongoing storm. The snowfall had lessened; the wind shaped it into piles against the sides of buildings and into snow dunes on the lake.

Out in the yard, the little white four-wheeler started with the first tug of the pull-start. I took off the choke and pushed it out of the garage. My cold thumb pushed the throttle to the end. The wind numbed my face. As I drove out onto the lake, the snowdrifts rose up to the height of my headlights.

My little machine strained in the cold but busted through and over the drifts one at a time until I came up to the iced-over lake. I could see the light blue of the frozen water—the wind had blown the snow off the ice and, on the side, a wall of the snow drifted up and sloped down like a halved mountain.

Cautious in the past, I never before dared to set foot upon the frozen Lake Minatare. I had been told too many cautionary tales, heard too many descriptions of foolish would-be ice skaters and sledders, listened too many times to the stories about what floated to the shore when all the water thawed. But that day was different. There was less water now, the lake a dribble, a large puddle, a surmountable obstacle. Sitting on the four-wheeler at the edge of the frozen water, that day was the day for bravery.

I revved the thumb throttle to hear the sound of power and resolve. The machine was willing, waiting to be called into battle. I circled away from the lake in a long arc to build up my speed; I knew it required momentum. I spotted my target—the bank beneath the sole eye of the lighthouse. I revved once again. It was time.

My foot clicked the gearshift down and my thumb jammed the throttle. I stood up off of the seat as I charged through one snowdrift. Second gear until maximum rpm's then third. Another drift laid to waste. Fourth gear and the wind drug tears across my temples into my hat. Two more drifts avenged. The lake approached with an unforgiving icy stare. Fifth gear and the last, largest wall of snow on the edge of the bank. That too was left bleeding and defeated.

Then I was on the ice and still charging, standing with one hand on the throttle, one fist in the air. Ahead of me it waited, a gaping mouth of jagged teeth. It licked its lips. I threw my head back in laughter and drove my machine through it with all the fury and honor in my blood, exploding through the wall and coming out over the center of the lake. Then I heard the ice crack below me.

The throttle held down, I looked behind me to see white lines spider-web across the lake, coming toward me, to the sides, not quite ahead of the machine but gaining. I leaned forward and crouched with my head down for aerodynamics, the pain from the pressure on my thumb sharp now. The cracks spread farther, all around me.

My little four-wheeler screamed in defiance until I was across the ice and safe, under the watchful eye of the lighthouse. I turned and looked out across the lake and saw the center split and break off into an iceberg and fall into the water.

Back inside the house, after warming up by the fire with hot chocolate and a blanket, I answered the ringing telephone.

"So are you coming or what?" Nate asked.

"I don't think I'm going to be able to make it in. My car's way too old for this snow."

"Are the roads bad out there?"

"Snow drifts up to my neck."

"All right. I've got my truck. We can come out and get you. If you still even want to, which you should. "

"I want to."

By the evening, when my parents came home from work, the snow drifts were six-feet, over my head, and the snow continued to fall.

"You seem to be in a good mood." Mom said.

"Just excited for tonight. Haven't seen some of my friends in a long time."

"I was thinking about that on my way home. Carrick, it took me almost an hour to get out here. I was going fifteen miles an hour. It's not a good idea for you to be out on these roads and I know you want to see your friends, but I think you need to stay home tonight."

"Nate's coming out to get me. He's got a four-wheel drive truck. You've seen it. It's big. He won't have any trouble."

"It's a *blizzard*, Carrick. People stay home during blizzards."

In a few minutes, Dad's Jeep drove into the yard and into the garage. I listened to the garage door closing then waited for him to come inside.

"Steve, Carrick thinks he's going to town tonight," Mom said.

"Right. Think again."

"Nate's coming out to get me in a couple hours, with his truck."

"Sure he is. Do you want to call him and tell him he's not or should I?"

He went to the sink for a drink of water.

"I was just telling Mom that this is my only chance to see all my friends before they go back to college."

"Who's having the party?"

"We're going over to Kendra's. We're just going to watch movies and hang-out."

"You're not going. Call Nate and tell him to save himself the trip."

"Why?"

"Because it's a blizzard."

I shut the door to my room and sprawled out face down on my bed. The wind regained strength and I looked out my window to watch the blowing white dust under our yard light. All the snow was good for the farmers but it was wrecking my night. I picked up the phone.

"All right, so my parents are freaked out by the snow and they want me to stay home."

"That's bogus. I can make it out there. You need to get out of that house and this is the last time in a while that you'll have something fun to do. I'm going to risk my life for you, so you better be there when I show up."

"If you park out there at eleven, and flash your lights, I'll climb out my window and we'll go."

I went out to the kitchen where they were sitting down to dinner. We ate then watched the television in the living room, listening to the wind blow. I didn't speak or react to anything for the four hours before they went to bed. All of my actions and words would have been lies. I can lie, but I don't when I don't have to, and because I was sure I would get caught, I tried not to insult them more than necessary. They would be mad enough when they checked my room after I left.

Staying up watching TV and reading, I waited until it was almost time for Nate to get there then went in my room and shut the door louder than usual. The wind seemed to shake the house. At five until eleven, I put on my coat and hat and stood by the window.

At ten after eleven I still stood by the window. Then in the distance, in swirling white snow, I caught a flash of red. Then it was gone. The wind rattled the windows. I unzipped my coat, it was getting too hot to be bundled up inside.

Suddenly he was there—a headlight facing the other way. He must have turned around. Carefully, gently, I slid up the window and crawled out. I didn't have to jump, the snow came up to the edge of the window. I slid the window down but it went down easier than it came up and slammed loud against the ledge. I froze as a lamp lit up their bedroom. I turned and looked and Nate flashed his lights again. I ran for it.

The heater was cranked up in his truck and Nate was alone.

"Let's get away from here fast."

We sped away but Nate slowed down as we cleared the lake.

The roads were white, windy, and covered in deep drifts. We drove in the center of the highway, busting through the drifts. There were no visible lines and we were the lone car on the road.

"I almost didn't come. But someone kept asking me to go get you."

"Who?"

"Don't worry about it. You'll find out when we get there."

Cars parked any way they wanted to on the street. Kendra's one-story house was in the center of a middle-class block—there was no fence and a barren tree stood in the center of the lawn. The snow covered the bushes, leaving smooth mounds along the side of the house. Drifts piled against the side of her house to the tops of the windows.

Her driveway had at least five feet of snow in it. We parked in the street. When we got out and walked toward the house we could hear voices and some singing, but no music. Everything else around us was silent. We climbed up a head-high bank of snow to walk across the lawn. The snow was cleared away in front of her door just enough to open it. We jumped down and went in.

Inside, the house spread out in a low-ceilinged living room with a hallway to the bedrooms. A projection screen on one wall played Kendra's home movies. There were clumps of people in most of the spaces of the house.

"You made it," Jake said. He wore a fur-lined trapper's hat with the ear flaps down and the string tied under his chin. He was drunk and his face was red. "We're having stair-sled races. It's a tournament. Get a partner."

At the top of the stairwell to the basement, on the wall by the door, someone constructed an eight-team bracket, drawn on the wall with black marker. One team used a silver, metal, disc sled and the other used a red, plastic, rolled-up-in-front type. They broke masking tape at the bottom of the stairs for a finish line. I asked Jake where the bathroom was and walked down the hallway.

The light was on so I waited.

Sierra and Lauren walked out laughing.

"Carrick!" Sierra said. We hugged. She smelled good. It felt like it had been a long time since I had touched another person. She stood close to me, her hips touching mine.

"Hey, come find us. We'll be here, in the kitchen, setting up the ice luge. Come thirsty."

Turning down the door handle, the bathroom light was on the opposite wall but I shut the door and locked it first so I had to fumble my hands across the wall space until I found it. I sat down to catch my breath. It felt as if I hadn't exhaled since we came in the house. But I wasn't doing that bad, the people around me were familiar and good. I still felt alone, but not uncomfortable. I had felt like that with people many times before. I took another breath, checked the corners of my eyes then went out.

Sierra waited for me in the hallway with a red plastic cup of lemonade.

"I thought you were setting up the luge?"

"I am, but I got you a little drinkie. That's cool of Nate to go get you. He said he had to sneak you out of the house but the roads are so bad, and I told him, I was like 'I don't care if you have to get a snowmobile and drag him out by the ears; you get him out of the house.' Because we've all been hangin' out this whole break and no Carrick anywhere. We used to be tight, remember? School's been great but it's just not the same. I remember when the only thing we had to worry about was whose parents were going out of town so we could have a place to party."

"Which ditchbank the cops didn't know about."

"Exactly. Now we're all split up. It's crazy, you know? Oh, and there's no leaving. Don't even think about it. Kendra took Nate's keys. She took everybody's. That was part of the deal. If you drove here you have to stay the night. All night. This is going to be the best slumber party ever!"

The house was spread out and I moved through the crowd with my red plastic cup in my hand, not starting conversation but not avoiding it, until I found Nate shooting paintballs at a white wall in the living room with a blow gun.

"Carrick, come join in my masterpiece. We only have two colors, blue and red, so we're more looking for shape, not color."

He handed me the gun.

"Drop the ball in the tip and suck it back until it snaps. Then blow with a short, compressed burst."

On the wall across from us, Nate had started painting the face of our king. I raised the gun to my lips and shot a red ball where his eye would be. I took another ball and made the second. I handed the blowgun back to him.

"Nice work. The devilish red eyes of tyranny. You're having a good time, right?"

"I'm so murdered when I get home."

"Relax. You're nineteen, what can they do?"

"Kick me out?"

"Don't worry about that. Did you see her yet?"

"Yeah, I talked to her for a while in the hallway."

"I thought she was downstairs."

"Sierra?"

"No, not Sierra."

I hadn't drank since Lincoln and the feeling surprised me. I moved slow through the house to keep my head until I found the cordless phone on the wall and took it into the bathroom.

Outside someone knocked and tried to turn the locked doorknob.

"Hey, Mom, it's me. Look, I'm really sorry, but Nate came and picked me up and I'm at Kendra's. I know you guys didn't want me to go, but his truck made it out there fine and now we're here and safe and I'm going to spend the night."

They were kicking the door and yelling.

"Carrick Williams." A sigh. "I'm very disappointed in you. You lied to us."

"I know. I'm sorry."

The person scratched their fingernails against the outside of the door and tried again to turn the knob.

She sighed again. "Look, I'm glad that you called and that you're safe. Don't drive again on these roads tonight."

When I hit end and opened the door Jake fell into me and then crawled to the toilet and began to vomit.

23

Acceptance among my peers required reassurance so I sought out encouragement. I found it at the top of the stairs to the basement. Two sled teams were untangling from a heap at the bottom of the steps and Lauren saw me watching.

"Carrick, you're next!"

Erin and Tyler carried the sleds up the stairs and I took the silver disc from Tyler.

"Oh, I want in on this." Sierra took the red plastic sled from Erin and we positioned ourselves at the top. "You're so dead, boy."

Lauren counted it down and we tipped our sleds down the stairs. We started out even until I leaned too far forward and mine slid out from under me halfway down and I fell the rest of the way. But I beat Sierra to the bottom by four steps. She aimed her sled then dove off and landed on top of me.

We were laughing as we lay there but when I stood up I stopped. Across the floor, sitting on a rug on the carpet, Maribel Carter sat cross-legged with John and Sasha, playing a board game. She was looking at me but turned her eyes way, tucking a piece of her hair behind her ear, when our eyes met. It froze me. Sierra said something I didn't hear and Maribel went back to playing.

"Bring the sled up," Tyler said to Sierra from the top of the stairs. "It's loser walks."

What he said half-registered and I drug the silver disc up to Nate. I turned around without responding to him and walked down the stairs and stood at the foot, watching her. She rolled the dice.

"Carrick!" Nate yelled. "If you're not going to go, get out of the way. We're coming down."

Maribel looked at Sasha and John, then at me. She looked down when she saw me watching her and drew in a deep breath.

"Dude! Get out of the way!"

She stood up then.

"I'll be right back," she said.

She came toward me, glancing at me as she approached then looking down.

"C'mon," she said, taking my hand, the shape and feel of hers familiar and good. I squeezed back. She let go.

We walked across the basement and turned a corner down a dark hallway then stopped. She squared up to me.

"What are you doing?"

I didn't speak.

"You can't do this, Carrick. You can't be the weird ex-boyfriend who stares at me when he sees me and doesn't say anything. That's too weird."

I looked into her brown eyes and thought about what I wanted to say.

She stepped up to me and made her hands into two kid guns then put them to my temples. Her eyes were clear and open as she pressed her nails into the sides of my head. Then she turned around and walked away. I watched her walk away, staring at the empty space, at the light at the end of the hallway, the phantom feeling of her fingers lingering.

After a few minutes I went down the hall to the bathroom and closed the door. I looked in the mirror, washed my hands, then walked out. The pattern in the carpet rolled under my feet, down the hall, through the basement, up the stairs. The front door opened to a solid wall of white.

"Dude, where are you going?" Nate asked. "The snow's up to

the roof."

I turned around and went to the sliding glass doors on the other side of the house but they were full of snow. I wondered how hard it would be to climb up a chimney.

"I just want to get out of here," I said.

I stopped at the top of the steps, next to him, and looked down the stairwell. I wanted to dive headfirst. I wanted to stop feeling as bad as I did. I wanted something to distract me from my longing.

"Get the sleds. I'm going to dominate your face," I said.

"Oh, bring it."

"I want the red one this time."

"Red sled, silver sled. Just bring it."

We lined up. Sierra stretched the tape across the bottom and Lauren counted to three. Then we tipped down and went. It wasn't close; I killed him. The silver sled was way slower and the only way to win with that one was bailing early.

"We'll talk about my trophy later."

I handed the sled to Sierra, resisting it at first. I didn't want to, I wanted to go back up the stairs, but I had to try again. I looked over and she was back on the floor, watching the dice roll on the board again as I came over. I knelt down.

"Maribel, can we talk?"

"This is a bad time. My hotel business is booming."

"I need to talk to you."

She took a breath then stood and pointed at her fake money.

"I counted that."

We went through the basement, I took her hand this time, and down the hall and into a room and turned on the lights. It must have been Kendra's room; there were puppies and flowers on the walls. Stuffed animals on the bed. She sat on the edge and I shut the door then sat next to her.

"Okay, look. There are things I need to tell you before it's too late...though it is already I'm sure, but I wanted you to know I care about you. It might be hard for you to believe but I do think about what you do, what you think, who you are. You started the process. I don't want to say you changed me, but you did change me. At least a little bit. I don't feel like I need to own you, to possess you. Love without ownership. I've always felt like when we were together we were getting somewhere, going somewhere together."

"I told you once and I still think it. You think about yourself too much."

"It's not that I'm so stuck inside my head I can't talk about you, or the world, or everything or nothing, it's just that I'm learning how. I'm slow. I've been trying to figure out what I wanted my whole life and I know now that I want to talk to you. To stand next to you. But not to own you."

I was looking at her. She was looking at the floor. I continued.

"Before, I had this filter, this inner...critic, I guess, that prevented me from talking in a normal way. Saying normal things. I never wanted to sound average, to sound common, you know. I thought I needed to be original, to be different. To never say a commonplace thing. And it slowed me down, that trying to think of something good to say all the time, when really, what I should have been doing was just talking...you know? Do you understand that?"

She smoothed out her jeans.

"First, Carrick, there are a lot of ways to be original, and not participating isn't one of them. That's just weak. It's hard to be unique, but it's harder to be unique and actually be a part of everything. Look, people aren't going to remember the average things you say, they'll remember the good things, but they won't listen if you never talk. That's all I want from you, to hear what you're thinking, to know what you want, what you feel."

"But I just feel like all my words are clutter if they don't mean anything."

"Words aren't the only thing with meaning. You can't walk around trying to be profound all the time. You can't try to impress me word by word. There's a lot more to it then that. I know I talk a lot, but I want to hear what you have to say."

"I know. I *know.* I've been quiet around the people I get close to my whole life. It's not that I don't have anything to say, it's just...I don't know."

"What? See, you have to be honest."

"It's just, sometimes I feel like the things I say aren't making anyone's life any better. That maybe they don't want to hear me talk."

"That's stupid. Of course I want to hear you talk. Why would I be sitting here if I didn't? It's because I think you might have something good to say. If you would just *say* it."

We could hear the sleds sliding down the stairs above us, the laughter. The basement shook when they went down, stair by stair. She tucked her hair behind her ear. I looked at her and she glanced at me then looked down. I kissed her. She gently pushed me back.

"This is weird," she said. "Let's get out here."

"Good call. Let's get out of this house."

"How? Have you seen it outside? The snow's up to the roof."

"C'mon. Follow me."

I took her hand and we went upstairs. They had quit sledding and were in the kitchen, where they poured peppermint liquor down three grooves they made in a block of ice into waiting mouths. We stopped at the coat closet by the front door.

"Bundle up. You'll need layers. Make sure you have thick enough gloves."

I started pulling snow pants on. She laughed then did the same.

When we were covered in clothes I opened the front door.

"We'll have to dig past the roof. Are you in?"

"I'm in."

She threw her first handful of snow at me and it bounced off my chest. I pressed her into the wall of snow facing me and touched her mouth with mine. The snow was cold but she was warm.

"We've got work to do, mister."

We worked and dug out a hole big enough for us to crawl into side by side, shoulder to shoulder. The snow we dug out melted on the floor of the house. It had come down light and was still dry and didn't stick together.

We climbed in headfirst and pushed the snow out between our knees.

After we went ten feet the light from the house started to dim. We had filled up the tunnel behind us and it was growing dark. We dug in front of our faces then, scratching at the walls, climbing up. As we opened the space above us the snow we pulled down covered us to our waists. We lifted our legs and the snow filled in the holes where our feet were and we stepped on it. It was getting hard to breathe and it was dark in the tunnel. We clawed together, faster, more desperate, digging then stepping.

"Are we going to be able to get out of this?"

"Keep digging up."

We stepped the length of our body twice but still did not break through—our breathing rate the result of our claustrophobic thoughts. The clawing and digging was becoming more frantic. We were breathing harder, using up the air, in the dark, the two sounds our breathing and our gloves on the snow. Then a change. We could see faint images of our hands, our shoulders, our chests, our faces, our whole bodies. Light filtered through white snow and we stepped up and our shoulders came out together. Blinding light reflected from the snow. The sun was rising in the east. It was dawn. We climbed all the way out and lay down on our backs in the middle of the yard, in the middle of the white landscape, in the middle of nothing, in the middle of everything. Everything was silent, still, frozen at the bottom of a lake. The cars were parked in the streets with no order, scattered like toys, sidewalks and streets stretching out for blocks. Above them miles and miles of telephone poles, electric wires—a silent communication grid. Across the horizon, at the edge of the land and the sky, a yellow glow grew, the light spreading over everything, over everything, everything.

The ride to the lake. Long looks, deep breaths, glimpses of smiles, familiar silences, comfortable postures. She was the one thing that I wanted. All the gates were open, the wheels turned to slide open the metal sheets and let the water rush through. People came together in long lines making hand chains. A wanted stranger closed a curtain in a studio apartment. A dark haired girl not unlike Maribel unfolded a blanket from her bag as the sun sank on the west coast, over the ocean, and in a white shirt and gold skirt spread it out on the sand to watch the sky turn red. A blonde haired girl at the table of a sidewalk café, drinking coffee, wearing sunglasses, crossing and uncrossing her legs, read her favorite book for the first time. A mother came home from a weeklong conference to a waiting family, a clean house, a set table, a dinner cooked by her husband. A father stood before his daughter with a clear expression of earned pride. A woman married another woman. Maribel took my hand from my knee. We drove on.

We turned toward the dock and drove down beside it, the trees to one side and the cracked lake to the other. We drove slow, the sun coming in through our windshield. The truck made tracks in the snow and, above us, the trees reached their hands up with white fingers.

We parked a short distance before the yard and got out. We met in front of the truck, our feet crunching in the snow. We walked together at a slow pace until we came to the yard.

The lights were off in the house and we kept to the side so they couldn't see us. Maribel opened the shed doors and I found the light switch. We took off our gloves then opened the two trunk latches in unison. The lid opened easier than before.

We took the painting out together, it was upside down, and set the end of it down on the shed floor. We spun the painting.

We looked at it.

"It's good."

"It's really good."

The painting, the two blocks of color had changed from the green and gold of the last time we looked at it together. As we stood before it, we saw it become the color of communication, of honesty, of a train to the ocean, a sign changed from open to closed, a commitment to peace, riding horses, a neighborhood buried in snow, effort, winter dreams, the light at the top of a tunnel, woven fingers, warmth, a child's playground, a sun over a mountain, an empty freeway, pulling a chair to a desk, kid guns, passion, riding four-wheelers across a frozen lake, making something, faith in another person, getting where you're going, balance, finding meaning, waking up, understanding, and the color of everything.

Acknowledgments

Thank you to Adam Gnade for nudging me to put this book out in the world with a proper layout and publisher. Thank you to Nate Perkins for deciding to take on this project and give this story new life. I wrote *The Green and the Gold* in 2003 when I was 25 and living a block from the ocean in Encinitas, California, looking back at the place I knew the best - Nebraska. The history of this book and its long path to get here is explained in Adam's generous introduction. Here's to good friends believing in one another.

About the Author

Bart Schaneman lives in Denver, Colorado with his wife Nammin. He works as a business reporter covering the cannabis industry. He was raised on a farm in western Nebraska. He is also the author of the travelogue *Trans-Siberian*, the collection of essays and poetry *Someplace Else: On Wanderlust, Expatriate Life, and the Call of the Wild*, and the novella *The Silence is the Noise*.

www.bartschaneman.com.

OTHER VERY FINE TITLES FROM
TRIDENT PRESS

Blood-Soaked Buddha/Hard Earth Pascal
by Noah Cicero

Marking a significant departure from Cicero's earlier fictional and poetic works, *Blood-Soaked Buddha/Hard Earth Pascal* is a lucid philosophical treatise. Rather than entertain dogma, Cicero approaches a discussion of Buddhism from the refreshing perpective of the everyman, providing a profound spiritual analysis as well as a sharp critique of capitalism. There are even some pretty good ghost stories.

it gets cold
by jasper avery

it gets cold demands a body that is both the haunting and the house, a queerness that is both living and dying. What can be gained by inhabiting this liminal space? What can the inhabitation of dying bring to the living? What can be done when it gets cold?

Major Diamonds Nights & Knives
by Katie Foster

Major Diamonds Nights & Knives is a poetry project modeled after a deck of cards. While writing this poem, Katie Foster felt possessed by a spirit who died in childbirth. She tried to tell her story as best she could.

Cactus
by Nathaniel Kennon Perkins

A correctional officer who guards the inmates that pick up trash on the side of the highway can't help but feel like he recognizes on of the inmates in his charge. RIYL punk rock, psychedelic drugs.

The Pocket Emma Goldman

Some great Goldman essays collected in one place. This book is perfect for carrying in your pocket so you can secretly read anarcha-feminist literature while you're supposed to be working.

Sixty Tattoos I Secretly Gave Myself at Work

by Tanner Ballengee

Ex-girlfriends. LSD. Motorcyle and canoe trips. *Seinfeld.* Skateboarding. Drunk friends and punk rock and shitty jobs. *Sixty Tattoos I Secretly Gave Myself at Work* is the most beautiful, the most vulnerable of punk and adventure memoirs. Each vignette centers around a hand-poked tattoo that the author gave himself on company time.

The Pocket Peter Kropotkin

Collected in this cute, pocket-sized volume are eight of Kropotkin's essays. The book starts with his indispensable article on anarchism, originally written for the Eleventh Edition of the *Encyclopedia Britannica,* and moves forward to expound on his ideas, which include prison abolition, syndicalism, expropriation, etc.

The Silence is the Noise

by Bart Schaneman

After a few years living in cities, Ethan Thomas returns to his rural Nebraska hometown and takes a reporting job at the community newspaper. He stumbles upon a big story when an out-of-state oil company pumps enough fracking wasewater into the ground to induce earthquakes. As Ethan learns to write he reconnects with a young woman from his childhood. This is a story about the complicated relationship we have with the places we know best, the pull of the ouside world, and finding something to love.

The Pocket Aleister Crowley

Famously called "the most evil man in Britain," Aleister Crowley's impact upon the occult traditions was nothing short of monumental. The selected works contained within this pocket-sized volume offer a way of thinking that is scientific and individualistic, but also deeply mythic and metaphysical, leaving room for both human intelligence and religious inspiration.

Propaganda of the Deed: The Pocket Alexander Berkman

It was July 23, 1892, and Alexander Berkman was planning to die. He just had some business to attend to first. Dressed in a new suit and black derby hat, Berkman burst into the Pittsburg office of Henry Clay Frick, the notoriously anti-union manager of the Carnegie Steel Company. From his pocket, Berkman produced a pistol.

This pocket-sized book collects the shorter works of on of the world's most influential anarchists.

The Soul of Man Under Socialism

by Oscar Wilde

"Socialism, Communism, or whatever one chooses to call it, by converting private property into public wealth, and substituting co-operation for competition, will restore society to its proper condition of a thoroughly healthy organism, and insure the material well-being of each member of the community."

Los Espiritus

by Josh Hyde

Four grandmas stop the passing of generational karma by interrupting a wedding with a funeral. *Los Espiritus* is an absurdist, spiritual romantic comedy with a heartfelt message: "How do we transcend our humanity?"

America At Play

by Mathias Svalina

America At Play is a collection of instructions for children's games. Part poetry, part whimsy, part despair, games such as "Freight Train Tag," "Baptism," and "World War" teach valuable lessons, such as how to play and how to be American. It is, Herclitus said, reality's nature to remain hidden, but its rules are easily observed.

The Pocket Austin Osman Spare

Working on the cutting edge of both magic and art, Austin Osman Spare developed a unique synthesis of older ritual magic systems with post-modern, erotic, and surrealist themes. His theory of magic eschews complex formula and ritual to favor creativity, spontaneity, and ecstasy, embracing artistic expression and alternative sexualities.

With a Difference

by Francis Daulerio and Nick Gregorio

Cowritten by poet Francis Daulerio and fiction writer Nick Gregorio, With a Difference is inspired in part by Rancid and NOFX's 2002 BYO split cover album. Gregorio has adapted 10 of Daulerio's poems into stories, and Daulerio has turned 10 of Gregorio's stories into poems. Like a vinyl record, the book must be flipped over to read both "sides."

Western Erotica Ho

by Bram Riddlebarger

Western Erotica Ho follows the author on a family camping vacation from Ohio to Wyoming and back while the Summer Olympics filter through news headlines across the country, and the Sturgis Bike Rally in South Dakota draws thousands of bikers to the Black Hills.

Las Vegas Bootlegger

by Noah Cicero

Ryan Neroni is a lonely lawyer with bad breath. All his life he's had everything handed to him on a silver platter, but after winning what should have been a career-defining lawsuit, he discovers that what he really wants is to drive contraband across state lines in a fast car with tinted windows. With the help of Theresa Barahona, an innocent and aspiring multi-level marketing entrepreneur, nothing can get in his way. Not social expectations, not the emptiness of the western U.S., and certainly not a string of surreal experiences orchestrated by a shadow organization known only as "the Committee."

www.ingramcontent.com/pod-product-compliance
Lightning Source LLC
Chambersburg PA
CBHW020105130625
27959CB00002B/44